"I'm not about to sleep with you!"

"You know you want to," Reece replied.

Darcy gasped. "That," she snapped, "is an incredibly arrogant thing to say."

"Maybe, but it's true," he returned imperturbably. "I find you quite incredibly exciting."

Eyes a little wild, Darcy tilted her head to maintain eye contact as Reece came closer...and closer. "I think you must be thinking of someone else."

Reece took her small face between his big hands. "I don't say things I don't mean, so shut up and kiss me, woman...."

KIM LAWRENCE lives on a farm in rural Anglesey, Wales. She runs two miles daily and finds this an excellent opportunity to unwind and seek inspiration for her writing! It also helps her keep up with her husband, two active sons and the various stray animals that have adopted them. Always a fanatical consumer of fiction, she is now equally enthusiastic about writing. She loves a happy ending!

Books by Kim Lawrence

HARLEQUIN PRESENTS®

2231—THE PROSPECTIVE WIFE
2256—THE MISTRESS SCANDAL

Kim Lawrence

THE PLAYBOY'S MISTRESS

TORONTO • NEW YORK • LONDON
AMSTERDAM • PARIS • SYDNEY • HAMBURG
STOCKHOLM • ATHENS • TOKYO • MILAN • MADRID
PRAGUE • WARSAW • BUDAPEST • AUCKLAND

ISBN 0-373-12294-2

THE PLAYBOY'S MISTRESS

First North American Publication 2002.

This edition published by arrangement with Harlequin Books S.A.

Visit us at www.eHarlequin.com

Printed in U.S.A.

CHAPTER ONE

DARCY slid her pink feet—the bath had been *very* hot—into a pair of slippers and padded through the quiet flat to the phone. It was nice to have the flat to herself for once. Jennifer was a great flatmate, but she thought silence was something you filled with noise—preferably the loud, throbbing variety! Music-wise the two were not compatible.

Propping the phone against her ear, Darcy hitched the towel wrapped sarong-style, around her slender body a little tighter and waited for someone to pick up. She was just about to hang up when Jack Alexander answered the phone.

'Hi, Dad,' she called cheerfully down the line. 'Is Mum around?' She eased her bottom onto the table-top, anticipating a nice long natter.

'I'm afraid you can't speak to your mother, Darcy...she...she isn't here...'

It wasn't the news that her hyperactive mother wasn't at home that struck Darcy as strange—her community-minded parent was on more village committees than she had fingers to count them on—it was the peculiar note that bordered on panic in her phlegmatic stepfather's voice.

Her post-warm-bath, pre-glass-of-wine, mellow holiday mood evaporated. Darcy wasn't psychic, but she did know Jack, and she had the nasty suspicion that the icy fingers tap-dancing up her spine knew what they were about.

Her heart was thudding as she lightly asked, 'What is it tonight? Practice for the carol concert or the church roof committee...?'

Jack would tell her what was up in his own good time—he wasn't the sort of man who could be hurried. An affectionate smile briefly curved her lips as her thoughts rested on the man who had married her mother—Darcy loved him to bits.

Darcy had been five and her elder brother, Nick, seven when Jack entered their lives. After a couple of years Clare had come along and then, much to everyone's surprise, the unplanned but much loved twins. The Alexanders were a tight-knit family.

'Neither,' came back the strangled response.

The line between Darcy's straight, well-defined, darkish eyebrows deepened; Jack sounded perilously close to tears. This, she reminded herself, is the man who delivered his own grandchild in the back of a Land Rover without breaking sweat. She immediately ditched tactful reticence in favour of the upfront approach.

'What's up, Dad?' she asked bluntly.

'It's your mother...'

Anxiety grabbed Darcy's quivering tummy muscles in an icy fist; eyes wide in alarm, she shot upright from her perch on the console table. All sorts of awful scenarios ran through her head and with some trepidation she put the most alarming of these into words.

'Is Mum *ill*...?'

'No...no, nothing like that; she's...she's...'

A noisy sigh of relief expelled, Darcy slid to the floor.

'She's gone away.'

'Away as in...?'

'She's spending Christmas in a...a *retreat* in Cornwall.'

'But that's the other end of the country!' Darcy heard herself exclaim stupidly—as if the *where* mattered! It was the how and why that were infinitely more important. Her spinning head struggled to make sense of what she was hearing and failed miserably. No matter what else was wrong in her life, there had always been a solid, reliable, constant…Mum… No, this just didn't make sense—no sense at all!

'It wouldn't matter if it was down the road; they don't even have a phone,' her stepfather came back in a heavy, doom-laden tone. 'I don't know what I'm going to do! Everyone's asking after her. She's making the costumes for the school Nativity play, the WI want two-hundred mince pies by Thursday… How do you make mince pies, Darcy…?' he asked pathetically.

'We've got more important things than mince pies to worry about.' As if he needed reminding of that! 'Have you any idea at all why has she done this, Dad? Did you have a row or something?'

'No, nothing like that; she'd been a bit quiet lately…but you're right; it must be my fault.'

'Nonsense!' Darcy meant it. The day she found a man who was half as marvellous as Jack Alexander she was going to stick to him like superglue!

'Apparently she needs time alone. Are you still there…? Darcy…Darcy…?'

'Sorry, Dad, I dropped the phone.' There was a distinctly surreal feel about the entire situation. People like Cathy Alexander didn't suffer from identity crises, they didn't walk out on their family with no proper explanation!

'God, Darcy, what am I going to do…?' She could hear the escalating panic in her stepfather's gruff voice. 'Sam, Beth and the children arrive from the States on Friday. It's too late to put them off.'

'No, you mustn't do that!' Darcy replied swiftly. Since Jack's daughter from his first marriage had moved to the States the opportunities for Jack to see her and his only grandchild were few and far between.

'Nick rang to say to expect him at the end of the week, and no doubt Clare will show up some time.'

Darcy permitted herself a wry smile—it was so like Clare not to commit herself to a date.

'Your grandmother is likely to drop in on us at any moment. Can you imagine what she's going to make of this…? At the last count we were doing Christmas dinner for fifteen people that I know of, and the Aga's gone out and I can't light it! I never did have the knack with the darned thing like your mother has…'

Darcy could hear him gulp down the line. She took a deep breath; desperate circumstances required drastic solutions.

'Don't panic,' she instructed her harassed stepfather with shameless hypocrisy. 'If I pack now I should be there about… There shouldn't be too much traffic at this time of night, should there…?'

'Your skiing holiday, Darcy!'

Darcy recognised a token protest when she heard it.

'I know how much you've been looking forward to it…'

Darcy allowed herself a final indulgent moment to wistfully visualise crisp snow-covered slopes, twinkling mountain villages and the hunky outdoor type she had been destined to meet amidst the après-ski *gluwein* before she squared her slight shoulders.

'With my luck I'd probably have come back with several limbs in plaster.' You had to be philosophical about these things.

Did her cancellation insurance cover family crises caused by the parent of the policy-holder unexpectedly needing to find herself…? Somehow Darcy didn't think so.

'You can't cancel,' Jennifer insisted a little later that evening as she sat on Darcy's bed. Darcy smiled and continued to replace the skiing gear in her suitcase with clothes more suited to Christmas in a remote corner of the Yorkshire

Dales. 'You've been looking forward to it all year. I don't see why it has to be you; why can't Clare go home to help?'

Darcy laughed. 'I don't think domesticity is really Clare's scene,' she responded wryly. Her beautiful, talented and slightly spoilt half-sister had a heart of gold, but she needed therapy to recover from a broken fingernail.

'And it's yours…?'

Darcy couldn't deny this. 'I'll have to learn, won't I?'

Jennifer, seeing her friend wasn't to be dissuaded, sighed. 'Well, I think you're being a fool.'

Darcy shrugged. 'So what's new?'

Jennifer's expression darkened. '*That*,' she said angrily, 'wasn't your fault!'

'Tell that to Michael's wife and children.'

This year Reece Erskine wasn't taking any chances. He was going to lose himself in the wilds of deepest, darkest Yorkshire until the so-called *festive* season was well and truly over!

So he didn't like Christmas… Why was it considered a crime when a man refused to participate in the manic few weeks that culminated in several days of gluttony in the company of people you avoided for the rest of the year?

Of course, the most insupportable part was the fact that everyone was so *understanding*. He refused to put on a paper party hat and suddenly he was failing to come to terms with his loss. He'd had it with pop psychology, no matter how well-intentioned!

After the debacle last year, when the girlfriend—and he used the term in the loosest possible sense—of the moment, armed with champagne, sympathy and a criminally sexy nightie, had tracked him down to the hotel he'd holed up in, he wasn't leaving any clues. She'd proved to be a scarily tenacious woman! She'd had her revenge, though; she'd sold the story of their so-called 'stormy relationship' to a tabloid.

Whether he would have been quite so keen to avail himself of Greg's hospitality if he'd known that the renovations of the big Victorian pile had been at such an early stage was questionable, but that was academic now he was here.

'God, man, you're getting soft,' he told himself in disgust. His deep voice sounded eerily loud in the empty lofty-ceilinged room. 'What's a rat or two between friends…? A bit of good old-fashioned frontier spirit is what's called for here. Who wants to call Room Service when he could pump up the old Primus stove?' His tone lacked conviction even to his own ears.

Having unrolled his sleeping bag, he made his way into the overgrown garden that stretched down towards what sounded like a river in full spate. He tightened the collar of his leather jacket around his neck; it was almost as cold out here as inside.

From the bone-chilling temperature in the old place even after he'd lit that smoky fire in the cavernous grate, he suspected he'd need to invest in a few thick blankets to supplement his state-of-the-art bedding, which might well live up to its press and be able to withstand a night in the North Pole, but the Yorkshire Dales in December—forget it!

He looked around in distaste at the bleak landscape. God, the place was so *grey*—grey and extremely wet! It was baffling when you considered how many people waxed lyrical about the area.

The periphery of his vision picked on something that broke the dismal grey monotony. Something suspiciously like a human voice raised in song drifted across from the general direction of that fleeting glimpse of scarlet. Reece immediately felt indignant. Greg had sworn on his very alive grandmother's grave that Reece wouldn't see another human being unless he wanted to—and even then it wouldn't be easy!

Reece had come away with the distinct and very welcome impression that the natives were hostile to strangers.

Eager to defend his solitude against intruders, Reece followed the melody to its source, wrecking his shiny new boots in the process. He discovered the clear, pure sounds actually came from just beyond the boundary of the sprawling grounds. He could no longer eject the songbird, but his curiosity was piqued.

His days as a choirboy enabled him to correctly identify the number as *The Coventry Carol*. How very seasonal; how very corny, he thought, his lip curling.

Acting on impulse—which wasn't something he made a habit of—Reece swung himself up onto the lower bare branch of a convenient oak tree. The identity of the owner of the bell-like tones was going to bug him unless he satisfied his curiosity. Besides, if he was going to be carolled on a regular basis it was as well to be forewarned.

From his lofty vantage point he could now see into what must be the garden of the sprawling stone-grey house that sat at the bottom of the lane that led up to Greg's investment.

In the summer the green-painted summer-house was a magical place, where wisteria tumbled with vigorous old-fashioned roses up the clapboarded walls and over the roof. In Darcy's childhood it had been the place her knight in shining armour was going to propose. However, the romance was purely a seasonal thing; in the winter it became a cold, unfriendly place her childish imagination had peopled with ghouls and similar nasties—it was still private, though, hence the bit of impromptu choir practice.

Her voice, never in her view solo material at the best of times, was every bit as rusty as she'd expected.

'I can't do it!' she groaned.

That new vicar, she decided darkly, was a dangerous man, who had shamelessly used his spaniel eyes and a judicious amount of moral blackmail until she had almost been falling over herself to volunteer to stand in for her musical mother and perform the solo in the Christmas carol concert.

It wasn't until she'd been halfway down the lane from the church that the full horror of what she'd done had hit Darcy. She'd suffered from terminal stage fright since that awful occasion in infants' school when, after she'd been given the linchpin role of the donkey in the nativity play, the strain had proved too much! She'd frozen and had held up proceedings until she had been carried bodily off the makeshift stage.

What's the worst that could happen…? What's a bit of public humiliation between friends…?

A loud noise like a pistol shot interrupted her gloomy contemplation of her future as a figure of fun. If she hadn't automatically taken a startled step backwards the large individual who along with a piece of rotten branch had fallen at her feet would have landed directly on top of her.

As it was, the summer-house didn't escape so lightly—the jagged end of the branch penetrated the roof, ripping off several tiles, and travelled downwards, gouging a nasty big hole in the side of the structure. But at that moment Darcy's concerns were reserved for the man lying in a crumpled heap at her feet.

She dropped down on her knees beside him; phrases like 'recovery position' and 'clear airway' were running through her head. Despite the first aid course she'd completed early that year, she felt completely unprepared to cope with an actual emergency now that one had fallen at her feet.

'Please, please, don't be dead,' she whispered, pressing her fingers to the pulse spot on his neck. To her immense relief, she immediately felt a steady, reassuringly strong beat.

Grunting with effort, Reece rolled onto his back. For only the third time in his life he was literally seeing stars. He ruthlessly gathered his drifting senses, the halo vanished and he realised he wasn't seeing an angel but a golden-headed schoolboy. Given the clear soprano of his singing voice, the lad had a surprisingly low, pleasing speaking voice.

'I'll do my level best,' the leather-clad figure promised, much to Darcy's relief.

'I live just over there.' The scarf she wore wrapped twice around her neck prevented her turning her head to indicate the overgrown path behind them. 'I'll go and get help.'

Darcy froze with shock when a large hand curled firmly around her forearm.

'No, don't do that.' He hadn't figured out the extent of his injuries yet, and if the boy disappeared who knew if he'd ever come back or get help? The kid looked scared half to death.

'Give me a hand to get up.'

He seemed determined to get up with or without her help, so Darcy shrugged philosophically and helpfully slid her arm under the shoulders of the tall, dark-headed figure.

It wasn't as easy as she'd expected; he might be lean, but her unexpected visitor was endowed with a generous share of muscle and there wasn't a single useful roll of excess flesh or fat to grab onto.

'Ahh…!'

The involuntary grunt of pain that escaped his firmly clamped lips made Darcy jerk back with a squeamish squeak.

'Did I hurt you…? I…I'm *so* sorry.'

If all he'd done was bust his shoulder he'd got off pretty lightly. Reece supported his injured arm with his healthy arm and hauled himself upright, ignoring the sharp, burning pain in his shoulder as best he could. Nostrils flared, he spared the hovering boy a brief glance. The kid had a soft round face, snub nose and big blue eyes, and he looked as if he was going to throw up—which made two of them.

'Not your fault,' he gritted. The knowledge that he couldn't blame anyone but himself for his present situation wasn't doing anything to improve Reece's frayed temper.

'Should you be doing that?' Darcy wondered fretfully, watching the tall figure get slowly to his feet.

The stranger ignored her query. 'Listen, I think I might have hurt my shoulder.'

From where Darcy was standing there didn't seem much 'might' about it. It was obvious he was in pain; it was also obvious he was more good-looking than any man had a right to be.

Her slightly awed gaze was tinged with vague resentment as she took in the impressive overall effect of the combination of square jaw, sharp high cheekbones, wide, firm mouth and straight, strong, patrician nose. Even if you took that rich, thick dark hair complete with auburn highlights and those stunning, thickly lashed green eyes out of the equation, he was knockout material; with them he became almost *too* handsome.

Those spectacular eyes were at that moment slightly dazed as he looked around, obviously trying to get his bearings.

'I've got a phone in my pocket.' Lifting his arm gingerly from his chest, Reece nodded towards the breast pocket of his leather jacket. 'Could you fish it out for me…?'

The kid was looking at him as if he had two heads, which, given the cautionary tales that were drummed into the youth of today about strangers, was hardly surprising. He attempted a strained smile.

'I'm quite harmless.' He used the tone he normally reserved for frightened animals—perhaps it would work on kids too?

Darcy almost laughed at this preposterous claim—no man with a mouth like his could be classed as harmless! She withdrew her gaze from the said mouth with some difficulty—it was, after all, rude to stare.

She took a deep breath; she felt oddly reluctant to touch him, which was strange because she usually had to repress her naturally tactile nature—men especially could take a spontaneous hug the wrong way, as she'd learnt to her cost!

'Inside pocket.'

Darcy swallowed and for some reason got a lot clumsier. Her nostrils twitched, and her tummy muscles went all quivery, her twitching nose detected a faint whiff of expensive masculine cologne, but most of all she got a noseful of freshly scrubbed *male*. He felt warm, and despite the sub-zero temperatures she suddenly felt uncomfortably hot; she averted her flushed face as her fingers skated lightly over the surface of a broad, solid chest.

The sad thing was this was the closest she'd been to a male since Michael—*How sad is that?* Perhaps I'll be reduced to tripping up sexy strangers so I can grope them, she reflected with an angry self-derisive sniff.

It was a relief when she finally retrieved the phone and held it up for his inspection. They could both see straight away that the mangled mess was never going to work again.

The stranger swore; considering the circumstances, Darcy thought he was quite restrained. She had no inkling that he was restraining himself in deference to the presence of an impressionable youth.

'You must have fallen on it,' she said sympathetically.

He turned his head stiffly, his green eyes gazing directly down into her face. 'Brilliant deduction,' he observed nastily.

Darcy coloured angrily; so what if it hadn't been the

most intelligent thing in the world to say? *She* wasn't the one who'd been stupid enough to climb up a rotten tree. Which reminded her. Why had he been climbing a tree…? His clothes, which she had noticed straight off were extremely expensive-looking, were not what she'd call accepted tree-climbing gear.

Some people never lost touch with the inner child, but somehow she didn't think this man was one of them—in fact, it was hard to imagine that he'd *ever* been a child. He gave the impression of having emerged into this world complete with cynicism and raw sex appeal.

Reece bit back the blighting retort that hovered on the tip of his tongue and forced himself to smile placatingly at the boy.

'Are there any grown-ups around, lad…? Your parents…?'

Lad! Darcy blinked incredulously. 'What did you…?'

She'd be the first to admit that she was no raving beauty, but although she'd never brought traffic to a halt, or reduced a crowded room to awed appreciative silence like Clare, she had turned a head or two in her time. *Lad…!* Nobody had ever implied she was butch before!

True, she hadn't put on any make-up this morning, and add to that the fact the yellow cagoule she wore was a cast-off from one of the twins and was thickly padded enough to disguise her unchildlike curves completely, then just *maybe* his mistake was understandable; especially if he'd fallen on his head.

Her lips pursed; for a moment she couldn't actually decide whether or not she was insulted, then her ready sense of humour came to her rescue.

I've always said I don't want concessions made for my sex, that I don't want to be treated as a sex object—well, now's my chance!

Having three brothers, she'd learnt at an early age it was better to laugh at herself before they had the chance.

'My dad's at home.' She couldn't resist the naughty impulse to raise her normal husky tone to her approximation of a reedy boyish treble.

She gestured towards the path half-hidden by a massive holly bush smothered with red berries. 'It's not far; can you manage?' she wondered, her eyes travelling with an increasingly doubtful frown up and down his tall frame; underneath that naturally olive skin-tone he didn't look a good colour.

'You'll be the first to know if I can't,' came the dry response.

'But your head's bleeding.'

'It's nothing.'

Darcy shrugged; if he wanted to play the macho hard man it was nothing to her.

'Be careful of the...' Darcy waited like a worried little mother hen as her unlikely charge avoided the motley collection of dirty boots, Wellingtons and trainers which always seemed to breed in the back porch. 'Dad!' she yelled lustily, preceding him into the rustic surroundings of the kitchen.

If he hadn't been clutching his arm Reece would have clutched his head—the kid's piercing tone had increased the throb in his head to the point where he found it difficult to focus.

Her three brothers were already in the kitchen, and her yell brought Jack in matter of seconds.

'Good God, what's happened...?' her stepfather gasped, staring in horror at the blood smeared all over her jacket.

'Don't worry, it's not mine,' Darcy assured him.

The stranger swayed gently; it was a development that alarmed Darcy. 'It's his,' she explained, placing a supportive hand beneath the tall man's elbow. 'Part of that oak tree next door fell through the roof of the summer-house.' She gently led her white-faced charge properly inside.

Reece bided his time, waiting for the tidal waves of nausea to pass.

'I've been telling the new owner's agent since the summer that thing was dangerous!' Jack exclaimed. 'Are you sure you're all right, Darcy?' He scrutinised her healthy-looking, pink-cheeked face worriedly. 'Hurt anywhere?'

'I'm fine.' Darcy unwrapped the looped scarf from around her throat.

'And you, Mr…?'

The dazed-looking stranger with blood running down the side of his face closed his eyes and leaned heavily against the wall. An anxious Jack looked to Darcy to supply the information.

Her shoulders lifted. 'Don't ask me—I've no idea who he is.'

'How come you were in the summer-house with a guy and you don't know his name?' Nick wondered, regarding the stranger with a suspicious light in his hostile blue eyes.

'I wasn't in the summer-house; I was outside.' Darcy kept her impatience in check—Nick always chose all the wrong moments to play the protective big brother; he was the most infuriatingly inconsistent person she knew.

'Doing what?' Nick persisted doggedly.

Darcy rolled her eyes in exasperation before returning her attention to the man beside her. 'You should sit down,' she said in soft aside to the object of her brother's suspicions.

'Give me a minute,' the stranger responded tersely, resisting her efforts to point him in the right direction. Darcy was a strong girl but she knew right away that moving this man against his will was beyond her capabilities.

'Harry, Charlie, could you give me a hand?' she called to her younger brothers.

The twins shook their identical heads in unison.

'We'd like to, but...' Harry began.

'There's blood...' Charlie completed with a shudder of disgust.

Darcy, in no mood on this occasion to see the amusing side of a pair of strapping, beefy specimens who came over 'funny' at the sight of blood, gave a snort of exasperation. 'You're hopeless, the pair of you!'

'Wimps,' Charlie agreed cheerfully.

Harry nodded his agreement. 'Maybe he's one of those contractors working on the Hall.'

'Nah! They've all gone home for the holiday,' his identical twin pointed out. 'Besides, does he look like a builder to you...? He's obviously loaded.'

Darcy was inclined to agree with Charlie, but she couldn't help but reflect that the injured stranger looked more than physically capable of the odd bit of manual labour. Her mind drifted back to the way the hard, muscular contours of his lean torso and broad chest had felt— With a muffled snort of dismay she brought her reflections to an abrupt halt mid-drool.

The tiny sound drew Jack's concerned attention.

She flushed uncomfortably, shook her head and silently mouthed 'I'm fine', which she was, if you discounted the fact she was sleazing over a total stranger who was bleeding on their kitchen floor. She grabbed a clean tea towel from the dresser drawer to stem the flow.

'Maybe he's the bloke that bought the place,' Darcy heard Harry suggest.

Reece, who was feeling less awful, noticed a little hazily that the notion seemed to afford amusement all round.

'My God, mate, but you've been done,' the instigator of the theory sniggered, digging his twin in the ribs.

Darcy gave a long-suffering sigh. 'I hardly think now is the right time for a cross-examination,' she told them repressively.

At first it had felt as if the room was full of a lot of people. On closer examination Reece now realised there were actually only four besides himself and the choirboy, all male. The two youngest, despite being almost his own height, were scarcely more than boys, and either they were identical twins or he was seeing double.

'Shut up!' With enviable lung power the diminutive figure beside him silenced the assembly. 'Let's not get sidetracked here; it doesn't matter who he is—he's had an accident. Charlie, go get the First Aid kit.'

'I don't know…'

Darcy, wise to male helplessness ploys, was ahead of him. 'First shelf down in the bathroom.' She turned to the younger—by five minutes—of her twin brothers. 'Harry, get the dogs out of here.' With a lot of noisy encouragement the dogs eventually removed themselves from the chairs.

Reece remained mildly disorientated while his youthful rescuer continued to throw out a steady stream of orders as if they were going out of fashion to everyone, including himself. The hell of it was he found himself obeying the kid and meekly sitting down in the larger of the two armchairs. The small figure was arguing with the dark-haired male around his own age.

'How should I know why he was up a tree? Maybe he's a tree surgeon…?' Her elder brother had a very suspicious nature and seemed to have jumped to the deeply embarrassing and bizarre conclusion that she was trying to cover up some sort of secret assignation.

Darcy couldn't help but wistfully wonder what life was like with a few secret assignations—alas, unless she could rid herself of her wholesome image and get herself a bit of glamour it seemed unlikely that she would ever find out!

'My name's Reece Erskine.' So much for anonymity.

Nobody started in recognition at the sound of his name—Maybe I'm not as famous as I think, he wondered. A self-deprecating little smile made his mobile lips quiver as he relaxed a little.

'I don't need to trouble you; if I could just use your phone...' His firm words only elicited a few fleeting glances of benevolent dismissal.

Reece wasn't used to having his opinion dismissed and he found the novel experience irritating. It was even more irritating that he didn't have enough functioning brain cells to demonstrate to them how very much in control he really was.

'Shouldn't we call an ambulance?' a worried Jack Alexander appealed to his eldest stepchildren.

'Was he out long?' Nick asked his sister.

'I'm not sure...'

'I wasn't unconscious at all.' Reece's jaw tightened; he might just as well have spoken to the brick wall beside him for the notice anyone was taking.

'It would probably be quicker to take him to Casualty ourselves.' Darcy held out her hand expectantly as young Charlie returned conspicuously empty-handed.

'I can't find it.'

She gave a sigh of exasperation and glared up at her tall young brother. 'Do I have to do everything myself?' she wondered witheringly.

To Reece's amazement, the big guy shifted uncomfortably and looked sheepish before he joined his twin at the far end of the room. He was finding the family dynamics of this noisy household deeply confusing. Maybe it's me...? Maybe I'm concussed, he thought. He closed his eyes and the room continued to spin.

Darcy took the stairs at the far end of the room two steps at a time. She tore along the narrow upper hallway, shedding her layers as she went—the First Aid kit was exactly where she'd said it would be. Why couldn't men find something when it was right under their noses…?

'Learnt helplessness,' she snorted in knowledgeable disgust, and Mum let them get away with it, she thought disapprovingly as she rapidly retraced her steps. Her respect for what her mother accomplished on the home front had increased by leaps and bounds since she'd arrived home.

She ripped the scrunchy thing that had slid down to the slippery end of her shiny pony-tail free and shoved it in her pocket before she gave her head a little shake and lifted her fine hair free of the collar of her ribbed polo-necked sweater.

'I'll just clean up this head wound first.' He endured her cleaning the small but deep head wound with stoicism. 'I think it might be your collar-bone.' Darcy bent over the chair, bringing her face almost on a level with his.

He didn't know where she'd come from but he wasn't complaining; she was a major improvement on all the brawn. He watched her narrow, slender hands as she set about her task. They were nice hands, and it was an even nicer face. A roundish face with a pointy little chin, a hint of sultriness about the full lower lip…? No more than a hint, he decided, revising his original estimate as she raised the big blue kitten eyes to his face and murmured… 'Sorry. I broke mine once,' she continued in a slightly husky, oddly familiar voice. 'I know how much it hurts. I think it'll be less painful if it's supported, but if I hurt you too much, yell.'

'I will.'

Darcy's eyes lifted; under the scrutiny of those wide-spaced blue eyes, Reece got that strange feeling of familiarity again as she gave an unconvinced little smile.

'A fine little nurse our Darcy is,' the fatherly-looking figure remarked fondly.

Darcy; where had he heard that before…?

'They'll want to X-ray you in the hospital, I expect.'

She was halfway through tying the supportive sling gently around his neck before a stunned Reece saw what had been blindingly obvious all along.

The schoolboy and the slender, but very obviously *feminine* blonde were one and the same person!

'You're a girl!' he blurted out unthinkingly.

The note of resentment in the shocked cry made Darcy's lips twitch and her stepfather's expression grow concerned.

'Perhaps I ought to call that ambulance.'

Darcy put the final twitch to the knot around his neck and straightened up, brushing her hands down the gentle curve of her thighs.

'I'm Darcy.'

'Reece,' he gulped, not meeting her eyes. Since discovering the gender of his rescuer Reece seemed unable to stop looking at her breasts; they were full, rounded and at that moment strained against the tight sweater she wore.

She bent a little closer. '34 C,' she whispered.

His head came up with a jerk; predictably she was smiling.

In someone more fair-skinned the deepening of colour beneath that even olive tone of his skin would have been a full-scale blush.

'Mr Erskine thought I was a boy,' she explained solemnly to her family. Having been the victim of this mortifying case of mistaken identity, she didn't feel inclined to spare her patient's embarrassment.

After a startled pause, this announcement was greeted

with predictable hilarity. The twins cracked up; even Jack looked amused.

'Now, there's a novelty.' Nick lost his habitual sardonic sneer as he grinned in malicious delight at his sister.

Not wanting to come over as someone totally without humour, Reece smiled—it wasn't the easiest thing he'd ever done.

Darcy wasn't a vindictive girl—she'd made her point, and she had no wish to see him squirm excessively. She decided to take the spotlight off his mistake.

'Wasn't it you, Nick who gave up your seat on the train to the pregnant lady who *wasn't*...?'

Nick winced. 'Don't remind me.'

Reece's eyes did another unscheduled detour—this time in the direction of her flat midriff. There was no possibility that anyone would make that particular mistake in her case. Her jeans were cinched in around an impossibly narrow waist by a wide leather belt, and the blue denim clung to a nicely rounded bottom and slender thighs... The more details he took in, the more he felt inclined to think he really was concussed—nothing else could explain the fact he'd mistaken her for a boy!

'I'll take him to the hospital.'

'That's all right, Darce, I'll do it,' Nick offered.

Darcy reached up and ruffled his hair affectionately. 'No, you've just had a long drive—I'll do it. Always supposing you two filled up my car last night after you used it.'

The blond-haired seventeen-year-olds looked innocently hurt that she'd raised the possibility they might have found a better use for her twenty quid.

'As if we would.'

The three older members of their family snorted.

'It's really not necessary...' Reece began, getting to his feet. 'I've no wish to impose.'

The pocket-sized blonde looked amused by his attempt to regain a bit of dignity. 'You've already imposed, Mr Erskine,' she responded bluntly. 'So you might as well get your money's worth.'

CHAPTER TWO

REECE levered himself into the cramped front seat of the Beetle. He rapidly discovered there was a soggy patch in the worn upholstery. A quick survey revealed the half-open window was the most likely culprit. He tried to close it, but it seemed as though the ventilation was permanent.

Reece, who liked his cars the same way he liked his women—sleek, racy and maintenance-free—gritted his teeth and settled back to make the best of it.

'I'll be with you in a minute,' the diminutive blonde promised, bending down to peer with concern at him through the window.

Reece saw she'd discarded the yellow cagoule thing in favour of more feminine garb—a dark ankle-length trench coat that billowed as she ran off down the steep path towards the grim-faced big brother, who, it seemed to Reece, was the only one of the family with enough common sense to view him, a total stranger, with even a hint of suspicion.

A heated conversation ensued and, thanks to the broken window and prevailing icy wind, Reece could hear snatches of what they were saying.

'Give me the keys, Darcy.'

'Don't be stupid, Nicky, you're shattered.'

'And you're not?'

A blustery gust snatched away the next section of the conversation but it involved a considerable amount of gesticulation—it seemed to Reece that his colourful neighbours favoured extravagant body language.

'What if he's a homicidal psychopath…or a sex maniac? Or worse?'

Reece's muzzy, throbbing head didn't immediately make the connection between the sinister character they were discussing and himself until the brother continued in a suspicious growl, '...And I'm sure I've seen his face somewhere before. Erskine...Erskine...why does that sound familiar...? Don't laugh, Darce, I'm serious. Your trouble is you're too damned trusting.'

Under the circumstances, it seemed more than legitimate to eavesdrop. Reece leant casually towards the open window but unfortunately a large dog chose that particular moment to poke his nose through the gap and lick him affectionately on the forehead. He withdrew swiftly to avoid any more displays of overt affection.

'See!' he heard the girl cry triumphantly. 'Wally likes him.'

He assumed the canine approval finally swung it because a few moments later the blonde came jogging energetically down the path towards the car. She fended off the affections of the dog, who bounded over as he saw her coming, and only clicked her tongue in irritation as she brushed off the large muddy paw-prints on her coat.

'No, Wally, you can't come today.'

Reece didn't think he'd miss the large, slobbering dog.

'Sorry I was so long.' Darcy's smile faded as her eyes collided with the large stranger's green eyes and their gazes meshed. His stare had a heady, narcotic quality, and for a moment Darcy was physically incapable of looking away.

A breathless, confusing moment later she was free of that mesmeric gaze, and other than a heart that was still thudding too fast and loud and a dryness in her throat there were no lasting side-effects. It all happened so fast she wasn't really sure in retrospect if anything unusual had happened—he certainly wasn't acting as if it had.

Naturally she was relieved to see that the clouded vagueness had gone from his eyes, but she didn't consider the cool, analytical detachment that had replaced it to be an unqualified improvement!

'I'm not in any position to complain…?' The fleeting smile might have softened his hard eyes but Darcy was making a point of not looking—she didn't want a repeat performance of that silliness! The little shudder that chased its chilly pathway up her slender spine had nothing to do with the weather.

'Darcy.' For a fleeting, selfish moment she almost regretted not letting Nick, even in his exhausted condition, drive him.

'Of course…*Darcy*. I'm in your debt, Darcy.'

Darcy could almost hear him thinking, Outlandish name…outlandish family. She had a strong suspicion that had this man not considered himself in her debt he would have had no qualms about complaining; he didn't give her the impression of someone who had a particularly high patience quotient. She just couldn't see him suffering in silence.

'I'm not keeping score.' She decided to make allowances for his attitude. I probably wouldn't want to smile either if I'd just bashed my head and bust my arm, she reasoned.

'You're just being neighbourly, I suppose?'

This time it was impossible to misinterpret the acerbic scepticism in his voice. She twisted the excess moisture from the ends of her wet hair as she slid in beside him. With a wet splat the hair was casually flicked over her shoulder. There was a faint puzzled line between her feathery eyebrows as she turned in her seat and levelled her thoughtful gaze at him.

'Is that so unusual?' she asked, unable to keep the edge from her voice.

'Only slightly less so than an honest politician.'

Reece had noticed straight off that at some point during the last few minutes she'd paused to anoint those wide lips with a covering of glossy lipstick, and the soft colour clung stubbornly to the damp outline. This evidence of female vanity amused Reece; it also drew his attention to the soft lushness of her mouth.

Through the miasma of dull pain he felt his libido drowsily stir. It was the sort of mouth it was a crime not to kiss. Reece shifted uncomfortably as she gazed trustingly over at him. That was definitely one for the modern-man-is-a-myth school.

'Well, it looks like your cynicism has survived the crack on the skull intact—congratulations.'

'You sound disapproving…?'

Darcy shrugged; she didn't fight with people who were in urgent need of medical attention—even if they were misguided.

'In my experience people rarely do anything for nothing,' he announced, authoritatively doling out some more of his homespun cynicism.

This was a man who had very definite opinions, she decided, and a strong belief in his own infallibility. Darcy was beginning to suspect it might be mixed blessings that Reece Erskine had recovered his wits—he was one seriously joyless individual. In a different situation she might have been tempted to put up a strong argument against this jaundiced slant on life, but under the circumstances she contented herself with a gentle, 'I promise you, I have no hidden motives.'

Despite her assurance, his silent response—this man could do things with an eyebrow that defied belief!—made it abundantly clear that he wouldn't have taken her words at face value if she'd had her hand on a stack of Bibles.

She found it increasingly hard to hide her growing antipathy as she carefully scraped a clear area in the condensation on the windscreen in a businesslike manner.

Reece couldn't decide if he was being reprimanded or

not. However, there was nothing ambiguous about her disapproval—the stuff was emanating from her in waves! He caught the full force of it almost as clearly as the light perfume that pervaded her smallish person—his nostrils twitched; it was light, flowery and vaguely distracting, but it made a pleasant change from the wet-dog smell that wafted every so often from the direction of the old blanket flung over the back seat.

He watched as she wiped the excess moisture from her face with the back of her hand; her skin was remarkably clear, creamy pale and very lightly freckled.

'She doesn't like wet weather,' Darcy explained defensively as the engine spluttered and fizzled on the first three attempts.

'Who doesn't…?'

'Bingo!' Darcy gave a gentle sigh of relief when the engine eventually came to life. 'She's temperamental sometimes,' she explained, banging the dashboard affectionately.

Reece wasn't really surprised that she endowed the rusty pile of metal with human characteristics—it was entirely in keeping with the sentimental, mawkish traits this girl had displayed so far.

'The heater will warm up in a minute,' she promised with another trusting beam in his direction—she wasn't the type to hold a grudge, it seemed. 'I'll take the back road and we'll be there in no time at all.'

'Good,' he said, turning his face deliberately to the dismal view through the window. He hoped she'd take the hint and leave him in peace, since there wasn't any place he could escape if she didn't.

The snub was deliberate enough to bring a flush of annoyance to her cheeks. There was nothing Darcy would have liked more than to let her moody passenger brood in peace; he wasn't her idea of the ideal travelling companion—not by a long chalk!

The problem was he'd had a bump on the head; for all she knew, he might have a fractured skull! If he dozed off, how was she to know if he'd just fallen asleep or lapsed into a coma? This alarming possibility made her search his face surreptitiously for signs of imminent collapse—she found none.

But she did discover that in the subdued light her passenger's to-die-for bone-structure had an almost menacing quality. Nick's outlandish hypotheses were still fresh in her mind, and Darcy reasoned that this explained the small bubble of anxiety which she sensibly pushed aside—at least she *thought* it was anxiety that was responsible for the adrenalin surge that had her body on red alert.

The idea of being stuck miles away from medical assistance with an unconscious man had limited appeal for Darcy. No, the fastidious and reserved Mr Erskine was going to stay awake whether he liked it or not!

Trying to keep her growing uneasiness from her voice, she asked, 'What brings you to this part of the world?' Only a comment on the weather, she decided, could be less innocuous—not that you'd think so by his tight-lipped, rude response.

'Solitude.' *Surely* she'd take the hint now.

With anyone else Darcy would have felt inclined to put down this display of boorish bad manners to pain and discomfort—*with anyone else*...!

He considered himself a tolerant, patient sort of bloke, but ten minutes and what felt like several hundred questions later Reece was having trouble controlling his temper.

'You can't possibly be spending Christmas at the Hall!'

He hadn't come right out and said so—actually the gorgeous but tight-lipped Mr Erskine hadn't come right out and said *anything* without prompting, and then it had been as vague and uninformative as he could make it—but by a process of elimination Darcy was now pretty sure the injured hunk was actually staying at the semi-derelict Hall for the duration of the holiday.

'Oh…?' Reece wasn't about to let on that he'd been thinking much the same thing himself. After all his furtive planning he was going to end up holed up in some tinsel-decked hotel again this year.

Darcy felt encouraged to pursue her point—by his standards, this response had been positively garrulous.

In the cramped conditions—the car hadn't been constructed with his length of leg in mind—he lost all feeling in his right foot. Reece slowly shifted his right leg, rotating his ankle. His muscle-packed thigh nudged against the blonde's leg.

A startled, gusty breath snagged in Darcy's throat. A sensation that was all fizzing sexual awareness and no common sense dramatically surged through her, coalescing in a squirmy mess low in her belly.

Help, where had that come from?

The momentary distraction almost had disastrous consequences.

'Hell!' She braked sharply to allow the bedraggled cat dazed by the headlights to cross from one side of the narrow lane to the other. The feral creature disappeared into the dark undergrowth. 'Whew! Close call.' Her heartbeat slowed down to a steady canter as they accelerated away.

You could say that again! The abrupt halt had sent Reece's head on a collision course with the windscreen—the seat restraint was the only thing that had stopped him making contact. The pressure against his damaged ribs was exquisitely painful. It was becoming obvious to Reece that his chauffeur was the type of bleeding heart who saw no conflict in risking life and limb to save a dumb animal—probably the less appealing the better.

'Are you all right?'

Now she asks! 'I'm fine!'

Darcy's dark brows shot quizzically towards her fair hairline; his taut tone had been several degrees to the right of brusque.

'You're obviously not.' No doubt such stoicism was admirable but in this instance not really practical. 'Have you hurt yourself some more…? Shall I stop the car…?'

And prolong the agony of sharing space with Miss Sweetness and Light? *Anything*, he decided, was better than that—even replying to her incessant questions for another five minutes.

She obviously wasn't going to be satisfied until he owned up to something. 'I jarred my shoulder. *Why* can't I be staying at the Hall…?' he asked before she could press the point any further.

'Well, leaving aside your injuries…'

'Yes, let's do that…'

Repressing the angry retort that hovered on the tip of her tongue, Darcy jammed her foot on the brake as the lights ahead turned red. 'And the fact that the place is uninhabitable…'

'I found it quite cosy.'

'It's Christmas!'

'Your point being…?'

'Time of good cheer and loving your fellow man… Does that ring any bells…?'

The cynical light in his hooded, secretive eyes intensified. 'And come the New Year I can go back to screwing the bastards…?' he queried hopefully.

The sound of an impatient car horn brought her attention to the green light. 'Are you always unpleasant just for the hell of it?'

'It does give me a nice glow,' he admitted glibly.

'I don't think you've got the hang of the Christmas-spirit thing, Mr Erskine.'

'It's Reece, and as far as I'm concerned, Darcy, Christmas is just like any other day of the year...'

'But...'

'...except, of course, for the exceptionally high hypocrisy factor.'

'You mean you don't celebrate at all?' Darcy knew that it was none of her business how this man celebrated or didn't during the festive season, but for some reason she just couldn't let it go. 'What about your family...?'

'I don't have a family.' Reece hardly even felt a twinge of guilt as he brutally disposed of his numerous relatives.

'Oh!' Darcy, who was pretty blessed in that department, felt guilty at her abundance. 'That's sad, but even someone like you must have friends,' she insisted earnestly. She heard his startled intake of breath. Oh, dear, that hadn't come out quite as she'd intended.

'Are you *trying* to wind me up?'

'Why would I?' Even if it was exhilarating in a dangerous sort of way.

'Sins of a previous life catching up with me...?'

Darcy repressed a grin. Sarcastic pig...!

'Maybe you *don't* have any friends,' she countered nastily.

'I have friends,' he confirmed tightly. 'The sort who respect my privacy,' he added pointedly.

'Then it's a religious thing...?'

Her swift change of subject made him blink. 'What is...?'

'Ignoring Christmas.'

'It's a personal-choice thing,'

'There's no need to yell,' she remonstrated gently.

Reece's nostrils flared. 'Hard as this might be for you to comprehend, I don't *like* the festive season.'

'It must be pretty spartan inside,' Darcy mused, thinking about the bleak aspect of the old Hall.

An image of walls stripped back to bare brick ran through his mind; the draught from the open window whistling down his neck wasn't the only thing that made him shudder.

'Depends on what you're used to,' he responded evasively.

He looked to her as if he was used to the best—of everything. In fact, Darcy thought, shooting another covert glance in his direction, she didn't think she'd ever met a man who looked *more* accustomed to the good life and all its trimmings than him.

That wasn't to say there was anything *pampered* or soft about him—in fact, the opposite was true. Even in his present battered and bruised condition it was obvious he was in peak physical condition, and he had the indefinable but definite air of a man who would be ruthless to achieve his own ends.

Of course looks weren't everything, and for all she knew he might be afraid of the dark and give generously to charities. Either way, why would a man like him choose to spend any time, let alone Christmas, alone in a dump like…? It made no sense…unless he was hiding out, or running away…? Perhaps Nick's suspicions weren't so crazy after all!

Well, even if he is a sex maniac I should be safe; he doesn't come over as the type who goes for women who can be mistaken for boys—*lucky me*!

Darcy gave herself a mental shake and shrugged off the self-pitying direction of her reflections. Whilst there wasn't much point pretending that physically this man hadn't seriously unnerved her, there was no point advertising the embarrassing fact—though no doubt he was used to women making fools of themselves over him. As the feeling was *obviously* one-sided, and they were going to stay strangers, there didn't seem much point getting bogged down with uncomfortable self-analysis.

'Well, obviously I don't know what the Hall is like inside at the moment, but I would have—'

Reece was not used to explaining his actions, and he decided it was time to call a halt to her interminable speculation once and for all.

'You do surprise me,' his acid drawl interrupted. 'I was under the impression the locals keep fairly up-to-date with *all* the developments around here. I imagined I'd discovered the net-curtain-twitching capital of Yorkshire.'

Two pink spots appeared on Darcy's smooth cheeks; she sucked in an angry breath and crunched her gears. The faintly amused condescension in his voice made her see red. Why not just call us nosy yokels with nothing better to do than gossip and be done with it? She'd have liked to bop him one on his superior nose.

'You'll have to make allowances for me— I'm only home for the holiday, so I'm not completely up to speed yet.'

'That accounts for it, then.'

Darcy's eyes began to sparkle dangerously; the man had a very nasty mouth and there were limits to how much she was willing to make allowances for his delicate condition.

'*We're* nosy? That's pretty rich coming from someone who was spying on me from up a tree!' She hadn't been going to mention it because of his injuries, but he was asking for it…

Reece, who hadn't been in a situation that made him blush for years, felt his colour rise for the second time today.

'I wasn't spying.'

'That's what all the peeping Toms say,' she cut back with a provoking little smile.

Reece gritted his even white teeth.

'I've been demoted from sex maniac, then?'

'You were eavesdropping!' she exclaimed accusingly, a rush of colour flooding her cheeks. Her memory in play-back mode, she tried to recall exactly how bad what they'd said had been.

'It was hard not to, the way you were yelling.'

'Yelling is better than spying,' she countered with undeniable accuracy.

'I was investigating the noise pollution,' he gritted with the air of a man on the brink of losing his temper.

At that moment they approached a particularly savage bend in the road. His knuckles whitened as he braced his good hand against the dashboard.

'Will you do me a favour and keep your eyes on the road?' he pleaded grimly as her smouldering eyes showed a tendency to linger indignantly on his face.

'It's so hard,' she confessed apologetically, 'when there's you to look at.' She sighed soulfully, placing a hand momentarily over her strongly beating heart.

Actually it was getting increasingly hard to treat the fact she was a long way from immune to his raw brand of physical magnetism as a joke.

He shifted in his seat once more, as if trying to alleviate some discomfort, and his broad shoulders nudged against hers in the restricted space of the small car.

Darcy was conscious of a fleeting feeling of guilt that she was being so mean to someone who was injured and in pain. The other feeling the brief contact created was less fleeting and much more disturbing; the fluttery sensation low in her belly went into overdrive, and pulses had started hammering a loud tattoo in places she didn't know she had pulses! Her palms felt uncomfortably damp as she grimly gripped the cold steering-wheel.

'Ha ha.' Reece's nostrils flared as he watched the provoking little witch toss her bright head. 'You were making a racket and I came out here for peace and quiet.'

She'd never claimed to be Kiri Te Kanawa, but a *racket*—charming! What a great confidence-boost just when she needed it.

'If this is a sample of your usual behaviour I think I can guarantee you that,' she promised him drily. 'It's true that in the country we do take an interest in what our friends and neighbours are doing; perhaps it can be intrusive sometimes…' she conceded.

Reece found his wandering attention captured and held by the dramatic rise and fall of her well-formed bosom. The fascination bothered him—it was totally irrational: he'd seen bosoms a lot more spectacular. He worriedly recalled reading somewhere that head injuries could totally alter someone's personality.

'…but I'd prefer that to indifference…'

'God!' Reece groaned as if in pain and rolled his head from side to side in an effort to alleviate the increasing stiffness in his neck. 'I knew I should have taken a taxi.'

'My driving's not that bad,' Darcy muttered truculently. The fact he was treating the journey like a white-knuckle ride hadn't escaped her notice.

'I'm very grateful for what you've done,' he ground out. He sounded as if each syllable hurt.

'Save it! I don't want your gratitude.' With an airy gesture that caused the car to lurch slightly towards the centre of the road she brushed aside his protest. 'We may be nosy in the country, but we don't step over sick people yet, or ask for payment when we pick them up!'

She shot a disgusted glance at his perfect, slightly bruised profile; anyone would think his movements were front-page news, the way he was acting!

'I wouldn't like you to run away with the impression I give a damn if you get triple pneumonia. I was just making polite neighbourly conversation to take your mind off your pain.'

'I'm not in pain.'

With a lofty sniff Darcy dismissed this transparent untruth. 'You don't have to tell me anything if you don't want to.' An expression of fierce concentration on her face, she stared unblinkingly through the rain-washed windshield.

'No, I don't, do I?'

Another five minutes and the hospital came into view. Even as he broke the silence, Reece couldn't understand what made him do so.

'I'm being a great deal of trouble.'

As much as he liked to give the impression he didn't have one, it looked to her as if the cranky Mr Erskine's conscience was giving him trouble—she was in no hurry to ease it.

'Yes,' she agreed sweetly.

Reece was gripped by an urgent and irrational desire to make those wilful lips smile once more.

'And behaving like an ungrateful monster.' His efforts were rewarded: her lips twitched.

'Such perception.'

Truly kissable lips; shame about the sharp tongue that went with them. A nerve along the chiselled edge of his strong jaw began to throb.

'I came here to escape Christmas…'

'You should have said.'

'Should have said what?' he demanded in a driven voice.

Darcy drew up beside the Casualty doors with her engine running. 'Christmas has bad associations for you, doesn't it?'

He stiffened.

She had spoken on impulse; now she wished she hadn't. For an unguarded moment there she'd seen something in his eyes that made her feel like an intruder. The moment was gone; now there was only hostility and suspicion as he scowled at her.

'What the hell are you talking about?'

Darcy shook her head. 'I just got the impression… Forget it; I obviously got the wrong end of the stick. I'll drop you off here—less far to walk.' She thought about leaning across him to open the door but, recalling what she had experienced the time she'd touched him, she changed her mind.

When he'd gone Darcy drove around looking for a parking space, and even when she found one she wasn't sure whether or not her presence would be appreciated. But, personality clashes aside, it didn't seem quite right somehow to drive off without even finding out how he was. The family would certainly think it very odd if she returned with no news.

It was with mixed feelings she finally presented herself at the reception desk.

'I'm enquiring about a Mr Erskine,' she began tentatively as she approached the smart-looking female who presided over the empty waiting area. 'I came in w—'

'Did you really?' The young woman blushed and continued in voice absent of wistful envy this time. 'I mean, they're expecting you.'

Darcy looked blank. 'They are?' she said doubtfully. It occurred to her this was a case of mistaken identity.

'They said to send you right on in. Rob!' The receptionist flagged down a white-jacketed young nurse. 'Will you take Mrs Erskine through to cubicle three?'

Mrs…? God, they thought…!

'I'm not!' Darcy denied hoarsely, but nobody seemed to be listening to her as she trotted obediently along beside the young nurse.

My God, this was so embarrassing. She just hoped Reece Erskine didn't think the mistake any of her doing.

'I think there's been a mistake,' she began firmly as the young man drew back a curtain and stood to one side.

'Here she is…Darcy, *darling*.'

Darling…?

'Oh, God!' she breathed, her eyes riveted on the bare torso of the man who had greeted her with such a highly deceptive degree of warmth.

He was standing there, stripped to the waist, in the process of zipping up his trousers one-handed; her makeshift sling had been replaced by a more professional-looking collar and cuff arrangement.

Darcy didn't make a habit of mentally stripping casual acquaintances, but it seemed she must have made an exception with him because she found herself comparing the reality to that mental image stored in her head and finding it had hardly done him justice. With wide shoulders, amply endowed with muscle in a lean, athletic, unbulky way, his body was way better than good—it was sensational!

Her tongue clove to the roof of her mouth as her hot eyes went into exploration mode. No wonder her emergency stop had made him cranky—there were spectacular darkish-blue bruises all the way down one side of his rib-cage.

'It looks a lot worse than it is,' he comforted her.

Blushing wildly, Darcy tore her eyes from his body. 'Good,' she croaked hoarsely.

'I could do with a hand here.'

Darcy almost choked when she realised he was talking about his zip. Eyes wide, she mutely shook her head. The alarmed backward step she took brought her into abrupt contact with a second person in the tiny cubicle, who until that moment she hadn't even been aware of. No, I was too busy leching over Reece Erskine, she thought shamefully.

'Sorry,' she mumbled incoherently.

'No harm done,' the white-coated figure assured her cheerfully. 'Just a few cracked ribs, lots of bruising and the dislocated shoulder, of course.'

'What?'

The doctor looked bemused for a moment by her alarm, then he grinned. 'I see what you mean…no, I'm talking about your husband, not me.' Chuckling over their crossed lines, the doctor held an X-ray film up to the light.

There was that husband thing again. Darcy waited expectantly, sure that Reece would take this opportunity to correct the error—he didn't, and her confusion deepened.

She felt obliged to respond. 'A *few* seems a bit vague.' Even as she spoke, she was overpoweringly aware of the tall, scantily clad figure who had moved up behind her.

'Point taken.' With an unoffended grin, the medic clipped the film onto an illuminated screen and pointed out the defects with his pen. 'One, two and here's number three.'

'I thought he might have broken his collar-bone.'

'I can see how you might, but no. It was a dislocation. Agony to pop back, of course.' The disgusting, bloodthirsty *popping* noise he made to illustrate the point made Darcy shudder.

'It sounds awfully painful,' she protested.

'It was,' Reece volunteered.

'We offered him an anaesthetic, but your husband *insisted* we do it right away.' The doctor hastily defended his actions. 'A few days and the shoulder should be back to normal,' he promised. 'Actually, it's on account of the head injury we'd like to keep him in overnight, Mrs Erskine, but he doesn't seem too keen.'

'I'm not…'

'She's not surprised, are you, darling?'

The warm, caressing note froze her to the spot without

the added trauma of hearing her addressed again as 'darling'. 'She knows how much I hate hospitals.'

She felt a large competent hand push aside the hair from the nape of her neck. Darcy's hair was plentiful and incredibly silky, but very fine and inclined to go kinky when exposed to moisture—it had definitely been exposed and right now it was a mass of crinkly curls.

Her breath expelled in a soft hiss as she felt the unmistakable touch of cool lips against the sensitive flesh of her exposed nape. Her eyes closed and the strength drained from her body.

The doctor only gave a slightly benevolent smile as he watched them. 'Of course, if he hadn't been going home in the care of an experienced nurse I'd have insisted...'

Darcy's eyes flickered open. He's married, married to a nurse, was her first thought. Then it clicked— Me, he's talking about me!

'Where are you working at the moment, Mrs Erskine?'

'I...I'm...' It was bad enough realising she had a whole new identity created by this madman without being expected to act in character too!

'Darcy is staying at home. Making a home is a full-time job as far as we're concerned, isn't it, darling...?' A firm hand beneath her jaw turned Darcy's head so that she was exposed to the full intensity of his green eyes. No desperate appeal for her co-operation there—on the contrary; if anything, there was a hint of challenge.

'*You're* a full-time job!' she breathed incredulously.

The doctor laughed. 'I'll send a nurse in to suture up that head wound,' he explained, scribbling rapidly on the sheet in front of him.

Darcy waited until he'd gone before she exploded.

'*Are you mad?*' she seethed. Why hadn't she just told the doctor he was lying through his teeth when she'd had the chance?

'Hush, *darling*, or they'll hear you.'

She saw that he was looking well pleased with himself—and why not? Her anger escalated rapidly as he calmly began to shrug on his shirt as if nothing had happened. The man had the gall to stand there looking as if butter wouldn't melt in his mouth, when... Her train of thought skittered to an abrupt full stop—it had been a bad mistake to think *mouth*; she could still feel the tingling area on her neck where his lips had been moments before.

'Let them!'

He directed a mildly irritated glance in her direction.

'I don't know what you're playing at...'

'Sure you do; you're not that stupid.'

Darcy's eyes narrowed. 'Let's pretend for the sake of argument that I am,' she suggested sweetly.

'I think I can just about make that giant leap. They were highly reluctant to discharge me without assurances I have someone responsible to take care of me. Whilst I could have just walked out of here, it seemed less stressful all round if I was married.' The longer he was here, the more likelihood there was of someone recognising him and then it was only a matter of time before the local Press showed up...in his experience these things snowballed pretty fast.

'And you thought of me. Naturally I'm *deeply* flattered,' she spat sarcastically. 'Why on earth did I have to be a nurse...?' she wailed.

'I thought that was a nice touch,' he agreed complacently. 'If the doc had been on the ball he'd have realised you're not old enough to be experienced.'

'You're mad...quite mad!' she announced with conviction.

'You're not a nurse, then?'

'Of course I'm not a nurse!'

'Just when your father said you were a great little nurse I thought...'

'I've got brothers—I can stick on a plaster. I'm not Florence Nightingale…!'

'True. Nobody with an ounce of caring in their body could stand there watching me struggle like this.' He stood there, one arm inserted in his shirt, wondering what to do next.

'If that was a hint, you're really pushing it!' she growled. 'What if someone asks me to do something…*nursey*?' she worried hoarsely.

'Is that likely?' he drawled, managing to project the distinct impression he found her complaints slightly hysterical.

It occurred to Darcy that they were drifting away from the real cause of her simmering anger. 'Don't try and change the subject,' she growled.

One slanted dark brow quirked. 'Which was…?'

'I'm not your wife!'

'This is true,' he conceded with an expression that suggested he was mightily relieved about this. 'I didn't think you'd mind—it's not like I'm actually asking you to marry me or anything drastic.'

'For your information, I've been proposed to *several* times!' she felt goaded into unwisely boasting.

'Congratulations,' he drawled, looking amused.

Darcy's cheeks were burning with humiliation as she discovered a major flaw in his manipulations. 'What were you going to do if I'd driven straight off?'

'I knew you wouldn't do that,' he stated confidently.

'How could you possibly…?'

'You'd be eaten up by guilt if you did. You're deeply into doing the right thing.' He made it sound like a flaw in her character. 'Be a sport, Darcy,' he cajoled.

'I'm not lying for you.'

He sighed. 'Just don't say you're not, that's all I'm asking. It's no skin off your nose. Walk out of here with me and then you'll never have to see me again.'

Darcy's shoulders slumped in defeat. 'I must be mad...'

A wolfish grin split his lean, dark face. 'Good girl,' he approved.

Further comments were made impossible by the arrival of the nurse who'd directed Darcy here originally.

'I've come to suture your head wound,' the young man explained.

Darcy took the opportunity to excuse herself. 'I'll wait outside.' Halfway through the curtain, she paused. 'Are you going to give him a local anaesthetic?' she asked the young nurse.

He looked confused. 'Well, yes,' he admitted.

'Pity!' Darcy declared maliciously.

The sound of husky laughter followed her down the corridor.

CHAPTER THREE

'GOODBYE, Mrs Erskine...Mr Erskine,' the young receptionist gushed breathily as she left them with obvious reluctance at the swing-doors.

Darcy gave a sigh of relief as the doors swung shut. The red carpet was about the only thing that had been missing and, given enough time, she had the impression the smitten young woman would have produced that too. At least she could drop the wifey act now.

'What are we?' Darcy grouched, intensely relieved to be out of the place and out of her role. 'Visiting royalty? Do you always have this effect on people?'

'What effect is that?'

Darcy raised a sceptical brow. 'Like you didn't notice!' she hooted. 'The woman was deferential, bordering on obsequious.'

Despite the enigmatic smile she received in reply, Darcy got the impression he was even less pleased than she was by the VIP treatment.

The rain had stopped, but it had started to freeze, making the pavement underfoot lethally slippery. Darcy moved cautiously past the men who were gritting the entrance to the hospital, smiling in a distracted way at them as she passed. The gravel was crunchy underfoot as they passed the tall, twinkly Christmas tree, and a layer of sparkling frost added to the festive look in a way that expensive ornaments never could.

She only just stopped herself mentioning how much she loved the smell of pine to the wet blanket beside her.

'Where are we parked?'

Even though she hadn't forgotten the tall, commanding presence at her side—chance would be a fine thing—she started when he spoke. It made her realise how uptight and wound up the whole play-acting thing in the hospital had made her. Her fellow conspirator, on the other hand, had seemed almost to relish his role, or maybe it was her discomfort he enjoyed…? Considering the glimpses she'd had of his warped sense of humour, the latter seemed the most likely explanation.

'*We…?*' She lifted her eyes to his face, but not for long—for some reason she felt oddly reluctant to maintain contact.

Like a silly, lust-struck teenager afraid to look the unattainable object of her fantasies in the eyes! Self-disgust curled in her belly. Grow up, Darcy!

By the time she had sternly told herself to stop acting so *wet*, he had paused under the blue-white beam of an overhead light and was making a careful minor adjustment to the jacket draped over his broad shoulders. His head was bent forward at an angle; she couldn't see his face, just the strong curve of his jaw and the sharp angle of his cheekbones, but even these sketchy details were enough to proclaim him as something pretty special to look at indeed.

'Are you going to abandon me…?' He contemplated his abandonment with what seemed to her unnatural composure.

'That was my plan, yes.' She could see the flaw in this plan even before he came over all pathetic and helpless.

'No wallet, no money or plastic. See for yourself.' He opened his jacket, inviting her to disprove his claim.

No way—she'd been there, done that and felt her hormones riot! She was not conscious of placing her tightly clenched hands firmly behind her back.

'There's no need to act like an endangered species; I believe you,' she told him gruffly. Her sigh of defeat had a long-suffering sound to it. 'Do I look like a soft touch?' she wondered, wearily running a harassed hand through her dampish curls.

Dark head on one side, he regarded her in a considering fashion. To add insult to injury, it took him bare moments to come to a decision.

'Actually, yes, you do.' She also looked extremely young, still full of youthful ideals, a soft target for unscrupulous operators—a student home for the holiday possibly...?

His own innocence and youth seemed a long way off at that moment. It seemed an opportune time, given the direction of his wayward thoughts, to remind himself how far removed she was from the females who temporarily lent a bit of variety to his solitary existence— Reece wasn't looking for anything other than temporary.

His candour made Darcy's face darken in annoyance.

'And you're the type to take advantage,' she accused rattily.

Taken advantage of by Reece Erskine—now, there was a thought! She was too busy being angry, flustered and ashamed of her thoughts to notice that a new expression had filtered into his eyes.

Soft... His mind seemed determined to explore this avenue and there was no lack of appropriate material to feed his interest—soft lips, soft curves. The compulsive nature of his speculation had none of the objectivity Reece took for granted in sexual matters.

Don't go there, he urged himself, repressing the sudden strong inclination to lean closer to all that *softness*, smell the flowery scent that enveloped her small person.

Darcy set off purposefully, reluctant to invite ridicule by admitting she'd forgotten where she'd left the car. She was too damned spooked at the prospect of being enclosed in a small space with him once more to think straight or accept defeat graciously. She heard his soft but firm footsteps shadowing her.

'You *said* I'd never have to see you again,' she reminded him crankily.

'I'm a great believer in telling people what they want to hear if that gets the job done.'

'Lying, you mean.'

Reece winced. 'I wouldn't have put it that way.'

'That I never doubted!'

Despite the fact she wasn't making any allowances for his delicate condition, his long long legs seemed to be having no problem keeping up with the cracking pace she was setting—*pity*!

'I'm not exactly thrilled to find myself obliged to beg a lift either,' he rasped huskily.

Of all the ungrateful rats! Darcy came to an abrupt halt and turned her wrathful gaze upon the tall figure who had almost collided with her.

'That makes two of us!' she retorted sharply.

Their eyes met.

It was at that moment Darcy felt *it*—*it* was a tense excitement so thick the air quivered with it, so thick her limbs were all but immobilised by it.

It didn't seem to be a one-sided situation. His burning eyes kept moving back to her parted lips as though they were being dragged there against his will. She felt as if she was being drawn in by that raw expression in his hungry eyes. The tightness in her chest finally found release in a fractured sigh.

The compulsion to reach up and press her lips to his was so strong her head spun. Would they be cold, warm...firm...? Wondering sent delicious little shivers skating along her spine.

She wouldn't do it, of course, because she wasn't the sort of girl who gave in to lustful base instincts...all the same, *thinking* about it—and she discovered her embarrassingly lurid imagination had a mind of its own—made her body temperature soar despite the sub-zero temperature around them. Her dry-throated excitement mounted with dizzying rapidity as her knees began to literally shake.

Seconds probably carried on ticking relentlessly away in the few moments after speculative green eyes had met startled blue—but Darcy was unaware of the passing time as they stood stock-still in a silence broken only by the distant wail of an ambulance.

No good will come of this, a sensible voice, to which she paid no heed, forecast in her head.

Reece felt his breath perceptibly quicken. Her mouth was just sensationally lush. The uneven sound of her breath catching in the back of her throat was driving him slightly crazy. He watched as her clenched fingers unfurled and she began to reach out...he thought about them touching his face...his hair...his...!

With a mumbled expletive he took a step backwards. '*Darcy...!*'

It was a verbal warning, the sort an adult gave a reckless child about to indulge in dangerous exploration.

Mortified, Darcy let her extended hand fall away, and she stood there feeling stupid and confused by what had just occurred—whatever that was... He had wanted to kiss her too—hadn't he...? It hadn't been a figment of her overheated imagination, had it?

The uncertainty only lasted a split-second; she hadn't imagined anything—it had been real. She thrust her softly rounded chin forward defiantly. As unlikely as it seemed, Reece Erskine had wanted to kiss her just as much as she'd wanted to kiss him! She raised her eyes stubbornly to his stony face and her heart sank—only he didn't now!

So he had gone off the idea; she was damned if she was going to let him make her feel ashamed!

'Darcy what?' She sniffed angrily. 'Darcy, don't kiss me…?' she suggested shrilly.

She watched his eyes widen as she gave an appalled gasp—*I can't believe I said that!*

'Were you going to?'

I asked for that, didn't I? What was she supposed to say…? Given a little bit of encouragement, *probably*…?

Darcy served up a withering look. 'What a tactless thing to ask,' she observed, resorting to disgust to disguise the extent of her dismay.

Spontaneous and asking for trouble would have been closer to the mark in his estimation. No wonder the brother wanted to keep her at home—if she was his sister he'd never let her out of his sight!

For the first time Darcy noticed the lines of strain around his sensual mouth—as if not kissing her hadn't been the easy option…then why…? A horrifying possibility occurred to her. 'Are you married?'

Unprepared for the tense, accusing query, Reece blinked, his jaw tightening. 'That's not relevant.'

Her mouth hardened with contempt; that meant he was. Not again! She didn't know who she despised the most at that moment—him or herself. 'To me it is!' she choked bitterly.

Reece gave an exasperated sigh; he could cope with a lot of things but he discovered—rather to his surprise—that being looked at as if he was some sort of moral derelict by those big blue eyes was not one of them.

'If it matters so much to you, I was, but I'm not now.' He saw her slender hunched-up shoulders slump in relief. 'Though why it should be so important to you I don't understand…'

And Darcy wasn't about to explain. Having an affair with a married man—even if she hadn't known he was at the time—was not the sort of thing she felt like sharing.

'I'd introduce the subject of morals if I thought you'd understand.'

'I don't see where morals come into it,' he drawled. 'You didn't do anything...'

'If I had...would you have...?' Cheeks flaming, she struck her forehead with the palm of her hand. 'Oh, God!' she wailed. 'Me and my mouth...!' How to take an embarrassing situation and make it ten times worse in one easy-to-follow lesson!

His eyes automatically moved to the object of her contempt. The muscles in his strong throat worked overtime.

'Yes, I'd have kissed you back,' he admitted throatily. The words seemed drawn from him against his will.

Her eyes widened. 'You would...?' She saw his lips twitch at the incredulity in her voice. 'I knew that.' A puzzled frown crinkled her smooth brow. 'Then why didn't you...?'

Reece's bark of rueful laughter brought her back to her senses—and not before time. He stared at her flushed face for a couple of moments before replying.

'You don't kiss married men; I don't kiss girls young enough to be my...kid sister.'

It was the very last explanation Darcy had expected to hear. 'How quaint that you've got principles.'

'It comes as as much of a shock to me as it does to you,' he assured her drily. 'It's getting cold out here.' He spoke abruptly now, as if the humour of the situation was wearing thin. 'If you really can't stomach the idea of giving me a lift back I should be able to make alternative arrangements.'

Darcy touched his arm; he didn't flinch but his rigidity didn't suggest relaxed and carefree—was it possible he was not entirely immune to the contact? This not unflattering possibility was heady stuff.

'How old exactly do you think I am?' Repressing a smug smile, she worked her way towards her grand finale.

Whilst it might have been wiser to leave him in ignorance, given the dangerous sexual chemistry in the air, she wanted the satisfaction of establishing herself as a mature woman of the world in his eyes. Perhaps for once in her life she wanted danger…? Her eyes slid over his tall, rangy frame before coming to rest on his face, and she gulped; he registered high enough on the danger scale to satisfy the most reckless risk-taker, she conceded.

'Nineteen…twenty maybe.'

'I'm twenty-seven.'

His chin came up and the dark veil of lashes lifted from his high, chiselled cheekbones. His narrowed eyes raked her face. 'Not possible.'

'Furthermore,' she continued, breathless after his intense scrutiny, 'I'm not some teenage virgin.' Like he really wanted to know that, Darcy.

'What are you, then?'

'Your best hope of getting home, mate.'

His mobile lips quirked; his expression was still rapt. 'I'd not forgotten that. I was actually wondering what you do when you're not doing the angel-of-mercy act.'

A wistful expression flitted across her face. 'At this moment I should be skiing.'

'But you were lured away by the glamour of deepest, darkest Yorkshire?'

His sneering irony brought an annoyed frown to her face. She took any criticism of her beloved Dales very personally.

'There was a family crisis,' she told him tersely.

'So they called you.' That would figure.

Darcy resented his tone. 'I don't mind,' she flared. 'Who else would they call?'

'You tell me. My recollection is a bit cloudy, but there didn't seem any shortage of family members from what I saw.'

'You don't know the half of it,' she mumbled. 'I get a panic attack every time I think about how many people I'm meant to be cooking Christmas lunch for.'

'Is this the same girl—sorry, *woman*, who considers every strand of tinsel sacred…?' he taunted gently.

'This is the woman,' she countered angrily, 'who is trying to step into her mother's shoes and failing miserably!' The instant the impetuous retort emerged from her lips she regretted it; she regretted it even more when she saw the curiosity on his face.

'Your mother's ill…?'

'No, she's not. She's…*away*.'

His dark brows lifted. 'Another man…' It might have been a trick of the light but Darcy thought his hard eyes actually softened. 'Bad luck, kid. It happens.'

Darcy was furious and horrified by his casual assumption that her mother would have an affair. 'Not to my family! My mother has gone to a retreat to recharge her batteries, that's all…' Tears prickled the backs of her eyelids and her voice thickened emotionally. 'And I'm not a kid.'

Reece looked down into her stormy upturned face. 'Want to talk about it?' he was surprised to hear himself offer; he wasn't prone to encouraging soul-baring.

'Not to you.' Darcy thought he looked relieved rather than disappointed by her blunt response.

'Fair enough.'

She eyed him suspiciously before she eventually nodded and blew on her icy fingertips. 'If the interrogation's over, perhaps we should get along before hypothermia sets in.'

Face burning with embarrassment and humiliation, she turned abruptly on her heel. She deliberately turned her face to the icy embrace of the cold north wind and, as luck would have it, found the car almost immediately.

'I can't find the keys,' she admitted after turning her pockets and handbag inside-out and upside-down.

Reece, who had watched her feverish attempts silently, walked around the car to join her.

'Might these be what you were looking for?'

Relief was mingled with chagrin as she saw he was indicating the familiar bunch of keys inserted in the driver's door. He pulled them out, and instead of dropping them into the palm she held out he placed them in a way that meant his fingers brushed against her wrist. The tingle that shot up her extended arm was neat electricity.

'Thanks,' she mumbled without looking at him. She couldn't decide whether or not that touch had been as artless as it had appeared.

He inclined his glossy head graciously. 'My pleasure.'

The fit inside the car was even snugger than she remembered. His head brushed the top of the car and in order to accommodate his legs he had to draw his knees up towards his chest at an awkward angle.

She went to turn the ignition key but he reached out and covered her hand with his, and if anything this time the sensation was even stronger.

Her eyes, wide and startled, lifted to his. 'What's wrong?'

Besides the state of imminent collapse of my nervous system, that is?

'This kissing thing.'

Darcy wriggled her hand from beneath his and clasped it protectively to her heaving chest. 'What kissing thing?' she asked, desperately affecting amnesia.

'You wanting to kiss me.'

'*You* wanting to kiss me.'

'That too,' he agreed. 'The point is, now that you know I'm not a married man and I know you're not a teenager…or for that matter a virgin…' A choking sound emerged from Darcy's throat. 'Incidentally we have that much in common. There's no actual reason we shouldn't.'

'Shouldn't…?' She hoped he wasn't going to say what she thought he was going to say—he did.

'Kiss.'

She almost kept the wobble from her cool response. 'Other than the fact I'd scream blue murder, probably not.' She sent up a silent prayer that her claim would never be put to the test.

'Ah…! You've gone off the idea… Maybe it's for the best,' he conceded casually, before leaning back in his seat and closing his eyes.

Just like that! Heavens, she didn't expect him to get suicidal because she'd said she didn't want to kiss him, but he could at least have the decency to look as if he cared! It was, she decided, eyeing his profile with loathing, a matter of simple good manners!

Darcy knew straight off she'd not fall back to sleep for some time—her feverishly active mind was racing like an overwound clockwork toy. She glanced at the illuminated fingers of the clock on the bedside table and groaned: it was only two a.m.

Her tiny bedroom set beneath the eaves faced due north, and the wind was battering against the window-panes, sneaking through every odd crack or cranny in the well-insulated room. The Hall wouldn't be well-insulated…

'Oh, hell, why did I go and think that…?' She rolled onto her stomach and pulled a pillow over her head to drown out the noise. I will not think about him, she told herself angrily.

Trouble was, she did.

Her family had been surprised when on her return she hadn't brought home the invalid to eat with them. Their collective comments to this effect had served to add to the burden of her own guilty conscience until she'd eventually exploded.

'If you want to feed him, feel free, but don't expect any thanks. Me, I've had enough of him for one evening!' she'd announced.

After that they'd let it alone, but she'd been able to tell that they thought she was being mean and she'd caught Nick regarding her speculatively several times during the evening.

Thirty minutes after she'd woken from her restless sleep Darcy, armed with a torch, blanket and a flask of coffee, made her way up the lane towards the Hall.

There was no front door to knock. The beam of her torch feebly illuminated a very sorry state of affairs. Horrified, Darcy explored further; things didn't get any better.

'And I didn't even offer the man a cup of tea,' she moaned, stepping over a pile of ladders that lay across her path. 'And why…? Just because he accepted no means no. If I find him dead from hypothermia or in a coma it'll be my fault.' The knowledge increased the urgency of her search for signs of life.

A room with a door seemed a logical place to look. Her efforts were rewarded with the sight of the smouldering embers of a large fire in the wide inglenook.

Tentatively she approached the large human-sized bundle on the floor. She put down everything but the torch and knelt down beside the figure. Her ears were straining for signs of healthy breathing—in her present frame of mind she'd have welcomed the odd wheeze or two!

One minute she was shuffling a little closer to the figure with her hand raised, the next she was flat on her back, pinned beneath a heavy figure. An ungentle hand was pressed over her mouth.

'If you don't want to get hurt, stop struggling,' an ugly growl advised her. 'Are you alone?'

How the hell did he expect her to reply with a dirty great

paw over her mouth...? It seemed her assailant's thoughts were running along similar lines.

'I'm going to take away my hand, but if you try and yell to your mates you'll regret it. Understood...?'

Heart pounding, Darcy shook her head as vigorously as her position would allow. If she hadn't known this was Reece she'd have already died of heart failure. To her relief the suffocating hand lifted.

'For heaven's sake, get off me, you idiot; I can't breathe!' she gasped.

'Darcy!'

The pressure across her ribs eased but he didn't shift completely. 'Of course Darcy,' she grumbled crossly. 'Who did you think it was?'

'A burglar.'

She heard sounds of him searching for something just before a strong light was shone in her face.

'Will you take that out of my eyes?' she pleaded, screwing her watering eyes up tight. 'I can't see a thing.'

She felt a hand tug at the knitted cloche she wore on her head and pull it off. The same hand ran gently through the soft waves that had been crammed beneath. Suddenly the pressure over her middle was gone, as was the hand... Disturbingly she had mixed feelings about her release; there had been something very soothing about those probing fingers—no, that wasn't quite the right word...

She struggled to sit up and managed it with both hands braced behind her for support on the dusty floor.

'I had a torch but I lost it when you leapt on me like that.' She squinted into the dusty corners, hoping to relocate it.

Reece regarded her incredulously. 'Well, what did you expect, woman, creeping up on a man in the middle of the night?'

Fair question if you stopped to look at it from his point

of view—something that Darcy hadn't done up to this point. She realised how foolish her impulsive behaviour might seem.

She watched nervously as he got to his feet and moved towards the fire, pausing to choose a couple of dry logs. The fire immediately began to sizzle as the flames licked the wood. Picking up a box of matches from the shoulder-high age-darkened oak mantel, he began to light half a dozen or so candles which were laid out there in various stages of demise. As they took hold he switched off the torch and slid it into his pocket—it came as no surprise that he'd been sleeping fully clothed.

'Don't you just love candlelight?' he drawled.

'Not especially.' His dark hair was mussed up and what had been the suggestion of a shadow over his strong jaw earlier was now a well-developed dark stubble. Neither of these factors altered the fact he looked devastatingly attractive—well, looking at him made her feel fairly devastated at any rate.

'Now,' he said in a don't-muck-me-about sort of voice, 'you can tell me what you thought you were doing.'

What had seemed a perfectly logical step to take at the time suddenly seemed extremely difficult to explain to her critical audience.

'If you don't speak I'll just have to assume you couldn't bear to be parted from me any longer...' he warned.

The satiric taunt made the colour flare in Darcy's pale cheeks. 'In your dreams,' she grunted, catching her lower lip between her teeth.

'Talking of dreams, you owe me one—you rudely interrupted a particularly...'

'I don't want to know anything about your dreams,' Darcy assured him, drawing herself up on her knees and dusting the seat of her trousers with a vigorous hand.

'Even if you were involved...?'

He seemed to take a malicious delight in winding her up. '*Especially* if I was involved.' Thank goodness she had a thick sweater and a windcheater over her pyjama top, because things were happening to her nipples that couldn't be blamed on the temperature.

Reece laughed then and went to sit down on an upturned packing case. 'I'd offer you a seat, only this is the only one.' He fingered the rough surface. 'It's the only table too, for that matter.'

Darcy gathered the drifting threads of her wits—she hadn't come here to talk furniture. 'I only came to look at you,' she gritted, wondering why she had ever cared if he expired in his sleep.

'Not touch…?' he muttered.

'Will you stop interrupting me?'

'Sorry,' he responded meekly.

Meek, him…? That was the best joke she'd heard in ages.

'I shouldn't have let you spend the night alone just because you irritated me.'

Now that she had his complete attention, Darcy wasn't sure that was what she wanted… She didn't trust that innocent expression in those green eyes either.

He rapidly proved her distrust was well-placed!

'So you decided to spend the night with me after all, Darcy. I don't know what to say…'

Her jaw locked tight as she tried to act as if his wolfish grin didn't do anything to her at all.

'I'm sure you'll manage to come up with something suitably smutty,' she predicted acidly, rubbing her sweaty palms against her jeans.

His low chuckle was not only genuinely amused, it was also deeply, devastatingly sexy.

'The doctor said you needed to be carefully observed. I just thought I'd pop round and see if you were all right.'

'You thought you'd *pop round* at,' he glanced down at the slim-banded wristwatch on his wrist, 'three a.m.,' he read incredulously.

'I didn't know if you could cope, with your ribs and the shoulder…' She gave an exasperated sigh. 'If you must know,' she said, gathering up the flask and blanket and thrusting them out to him, 'I was worried about you.'

Reece looked from her angry, flushed face to the offerings in her hand and back again. 'I'm touched.'

'There's no need,' she said with dignity, 'to be sarcastic.'

'I'm not.'

Darcy tapped a pearly fingertip nervously against a white tooth and eyed him with an exasperated frown. 'It's perfectly simple,' she began to explain patiently. 'I was lying there, listening to the wind, thinking about you…'

'Snap.'

It took two seconds' exposure to his wickedly explicit eyes to extinguish the innocent look of enquiry on her face. 'I wasn't doing *that* sort of thinking,' she gasped, horrified.

'What sort of thinking would that be, Darcy…?'

'If you'd got ill in the night nobody would have known. I would have felt responsible.'

'You've got a thing about responsibility, haven't you, Darcy?' he mused softly. 'Don't you ever get the urge to do something irresponsible?' The humour faded abruptly from his eyes.

Darcy swallowed, and waited for the worst of the spasms in her belly to pass. It must be the candles, she reasoned desperately. 'No, never.' Her stern denial emerged as a hollow whisper.

Her fingers, still curled around the blanket and Thermos, trembled. It didn't occur to her to release her grip on them as he pulled them—and her—slowly towards him. Finally he removed them from her weak grasp and placed them on the floor. His eyes never left hers all the time.

An image of the livid bruising she'd seen on his body came into her head, but her imagination didn't limit itself to damage; it conjured up some impressive muscles, smooth olive-toned flesh and crisp body hair too. She ran the tip of her tongue over her dry lips to lubricate them and gave her head a tiny shake, but neither act totally dispelled the disturbing image.

'Did I hurt you?' she asked hoarsely. She knew she hadn't been a submissive victim.

He touched the side of her face softly and sent an illicit little shiver through the tense body. Darcy couldn't afford the time to worry if the tremor had been transmitted through his fingertips—it was taking all her energy convincing her knees they didn't want to fold under her. To make matters infinitely worse, the debilitating weakness wasn't just affecting her limbs…at best, her brain was functioning on a very basic, fuzzy level.

'Do you want to?' Finger on the angle of her jaw, he tilted her face up to his.

Darcy shook her head—she didn't want to think about what she'd like to do to him; it wasn't decent. His face was swimming in and out of focus as she stared back at him.

'I don't like hurting people. Do you…?'

Reece didn't reply; he simply took her by the shoulders and drew her unresisting body towards him, parting his thighs to let her rest within their confining circle.

'Are you quite sure that concern for my health was the only reason you came here, Darcy…?'

She had to do something to throw cold water on the escalating intimacy and danger of a situation that was fast getting out of hand.

'What other reason could there be?'

Underneath the faint antiseptic hospital scent and a distinctive male fragrance she could smell him—not just his soap or cologne, but *him*! Panic was just a heartbeat away—or was it capitulation she could sense…?

'This one…' His intention was written clear on his dark, impassioned features.

Desperation and panic flared in her wide eyes just before they reflexly closed. The uncoordinated flailing movements of her hands brought them in contact with the iron-hard thighs pressed either side of her hips; she froze and her fingers spasmed, relaxed, then tentatively spread out over the hard-muscled expanse.

'That's good,' he approved.

Darcy gave a sigh; it was. She felt his breath as it moved over her cheek, felt it tease the quivering line of her trembling lips in the moment before his lips purposefully parted hers. The sensual, silken, smooth stab of his tongue melted her last resistance.

Darcy gave a lost little cry and sank deeper into the seductive velvet blackness inside her head. The explosive force of his hunger was something she'd never encountered before. Almost more shocking was the equally unexpected raw response that uncoiled within her. She gave herself up totally to the seductive exploration, only stopping when she could no longer breathe.

They drew apart, but not very far. Her forehead was resting against his, her fingers were twisted in the glossy strands of his dark hair.

'I forgive you totally for waking me up.'

And, given he kissed like an angel, she was prepared to forgive him for sounding so smug. He knew all the moves all right; even now Darcy didn't want to admit even to herself that it wasn't simple slick technique that had made her respond to him that way.

'Ever undressed inside a sleeping bag?'

Darcy stiffened slightly but didn't draw back. She only

had herself to blame for this situation—if she hadn't kissed him back like that…

'Isn't that a bit of a leap from a kiss?'

'There are kisses and then again there are *kisses*.'

Again he was right. Until that particular moment Darcy hadn't known how great the gap between the two was. She was pink all over already, and the shade deepened perceptively as she encountered the sensuous warmth of his eyes.

'It's a challenging proposition…' she admitted, a responsive smile in her voice. Yesterday she would have laughed her socks off if someone had suggested she would be seriously considering sleeping with a man she barely knew.

'I can hear a "but" coming on,' Reece predicted gloomily.

Reluctantly Darcy released her hold on his hair and straightened up. She became aware for the first time that at some point during the embrace Reece had removed her windcheater. She stood there shivering, but not from cold.

'I think it would be a safer bet all round if you invest in a heated blanket,' she explained regretfully.

'No electricity.' His gesture caused the candles to flicker and dance in the draught he created. 'And if you're worried on a safety basis I'm a prepared sort of guy.'

'I wasn't.'

'You ought to be; you don't know me.'

She blinked. Is he lecturing *me* on safe sex…? 'Which is one of the reasons I'm not about to sleep with you.'

'The others being…?'

'You have several broken bones.'

Reece impatiently disposed of this objection. 'We can work around that.'

Just imagining what 'working around' might involve made her skin burn.

'You know you want to.'

Darcy gasped. 'That,' she bit back with tremulous contempt, 'is an incredibly arrogant thing to say.'

'Maybe, but it's true,' he returned imperturbably.

'What are you doing...?' she squawked as he got to his feet.

'I can't make love to you if we're on opposite sides of the room.'

This would have been even truer if I had stayed safely tucked up in my own bed—only I didn't. Why didn't I...? Did I want this to happen...? She shook her head in feverish denial but the idea clung stubbornly on.

'I find you quite incredibly exciting.'

His honeyed drawl froze her to the spot, the dark reckless glow in his eyes liquefied her bones, and held her there. Eyes a little wild, she tilted her head to maintain eye contact as he came closer...and closer.

'I think you must be thinking of someone else...'

'You smell like summer.'

'I do...? When you said we could work around it...are you sure...?'

Reece took her small face between his big hands. 'I don't say things I don't mean.'

'You're quite sure...' Darcy felt his low laughter against her ear, smelt the male muskiness of his arousal.

'Shut up and kiss me, woman.'

CHAPTER FOUR

THE impetus of the kiss made them stagger backwards into the makeshift table. A small bottle of tablets fell onto the dusty floor; Darcy automatically tried to avoid stepping onto the contents.

'Your painkillers…' Fortunately the bottle of whisky set beside it on the table hadn't fallen.

The arm around her waist didn't slacken.

'To hell with them,' he slurred.

'Good God!' she gasped. 'You've mixed tablets with booze, haven't you?' she accused hoarsely. 'That explains it.'

'Explains what?' He didn't sound terribly interested in her reply.

'This!' she indited shakily, stabbing a finger at her chest and discovering in the process that at some point during the kiss he'd managed to remove her sweater.

If undressing women ever became an Olympic event he would win gold with one hand tied behind his back—quite literally, she thought, her eyes sliding to his immobilised arm.

Flushing deeply, she gathered the lightly elasticated neckline of her pyjama top in one fist, which didn't so much conceal what was going on underneath the thin, silky fabric as draw his hot-eyed attention to it.

'I've no idea what you're talking about, but hell, you taste good.' He pushed a hank of her silky hair aside to press an open-mouthed kiss to the pulse point on her neck.

Darcy's head fell back and she groaned, the sensual shock of his touch juddering through her responsive body.

'You don't understand.' She valiantly struggled past the passion barrier to make him listen.

'Reece, I think it's probable you're having a reaction to your medication.' Depressing as it was, it did perfectly explain away the inexplicable—a man like him being so deeply in lust with an average type like herself.

'So that's what this is.' He firmly unglued her fingers and peered down the open neckline; what he saw seemed to afford him considerable pleasure.

She got even hotter. 'I don't think you're taking this seriously.'

'Believe me,' he grated hoarsely, 'I'm taking this very seriously.'

'You don't really want me,' she whimpered.

Reece's jaw tightened. 'Is that a fact…?' He slid the silky fabric clear down her shoulders and with a muffled groan pressed his lips to the heaving contours he'd revealed. 'Absolutely incredible…'

'Sweet…sweet…mercy…' Darcy tried to regroup but it was an uphill battle. His tongue had begun to travel very slowly over the slope of one breast. Did it really matter that he wasn't in full possession of his senses…? *'Listen!'* Fingers in his hair, she pulled his head back.

'What the hell's wrong now?' There was a light sheen of sweat covering his taut, lean features, the dampness extending down the glistening column of his throat. His hot eyes kept sliding from her face in the general direction of her heaving breasts.

'It's the medication. I think you've had some sort of reaction to it. You can't take alcohol with some sorts of analgesia. That's why you're acting like this.' Miserably Darcy brushed a strand of hair from her damp face and found she couldn't look him in the eyes—it was too humiliating… Her body was literally throbbing with arousal, aching for his touch.

'You can't think of any other reason...?' The blood in her temples roared as his eyes slid in hot, sensual appraisal over her body. 'A reason like I'm sexually attracted to you!' She audibly caught her breath. 'A reason like I've been lying here alone all night, wondering what it would be like to have you beside me, warm and soft, to be inside you. Then you're here...' His throat muscles worked. 'And you want to stay.' He smiled with grim satisfaction when she didn't respond to the challenge.

Darcy couldn't speak; the sound of his low, vibrantly masculine voice saying things no man had ever said to her was like a fist tightening inside her belly. She felt light-headed and dizzy and her blood seemed to hum hotly, pooling; the ache between her thighs was so intense she could hardly stand up, and, her breathing shallow and fast, she stared breathlessly up at him.

'But the—'

'Paracetamol. You can buy it anywhere over the counter.' His sensuous lips curled contemptuously as her eyes widened. 'The doc wanted to give me something stronger but I've never been keen on having my senses dulled.'

'Then this is...'

Reece nodded. 'The real thing. Unless you're going to tell me you're taking hallucinogenic drugs?'

The dazed look still in her eyes, she shook her head vigorously.

'Does this feel real enough for you?' he asked, pressing his lean, hard body tight against hers.

Darcy could feel him, thick and hard, pressing into the softness of her belly. 'It...you feel incredible,' she gasped.

'Take my shirt off, Darcy?'

'Because of your shoulder.'

'Because I want you to.'

That seemed a good enough reason to Darcy.

Her hands were shaking as one by one she slid free the buttons and pushed the soft cord fabric aside to reveal his broad chest and flat belly. Expression rapt, she spread her fingers and felt the fine muscles just beneath the surface of his taut skin twitch and tighten.

Her hair looked silver by candlelight and all Reece could see of her as she leant closer was the top of her head and the exposed nape of her slender neck. It wasn't an area he'd previously considered erotic—was it napes in general or this nape in particular…? That was a question for later—right now he needed to assuage the fire in his blood, the ache in his loins.

A deep line bisected her smooth brow as she examined the bruised area. 'Tell me if I hurt you,' she whispered, tracing a line across his belly with her fingernail.

'I'm hurting,' he told her thickly.

Alarmed, she raised her eyes questioningly to his. 'Where…?' she began. She saw the expression on his face and her voice faded away.

'Here…' he took her hand and showed her '…here and here,' he elaborated thickly.

Darcy whimpered, the last remnants of her control evaporating.

'I want to see you. Take your clothes off for me. All of them.'

Not doing as he requested—or was it a demand?—was never an option. Like someone in a dream she crossed her arms and began to lift the hem of her top up over her smooth stomach.

'And, Darcy…?'

She paused.

'Look at me.'

Darcy did. She could hear the harsh, uneven sound of his breathing, loud in the quiet room. Even in this light she could make out a definite flush of colour along his slashing cheekbones and the fire in his eyes— Did I really put it there…? How strange…how marvellous.

Their eyes locked, and her anxiety was instantly soothed; he looked just as needy as she felt. Despite the new confidence, her hands trembled uncontrollably as she did as he had bid. It was no slow, seductive striptease because even with a fire now blazing in the hearth it didn't seem such a good idea to linger over disrobing.

'You're beautiful.' She almost believed him.

He closed the small gap between them. Where he touched her Darcy's skin tingled, and pretty soon she tingled all over. 'And cold.' He began to briskly massage her cold extremities. 'Come on, get in here.' Taking her by the hand, he led her towards the sleeping bag and blankets.

The cotton lining still retained the last remnants of his body heat. Darcy drew her knees up to her chin and waited for him to join her, anticipation pumping darkly though her. She watched as he shed his clothes, ripping the shirt as he tried to ease it too quickly over his injured arm; he was lean, lovely and very, *very* aroused.

He was actually so beautiful she wanted to cry—she *was* crying, hot tears sliding over her cheeks. He wiped away the dampness with his thumb when he finally came to join her but didn't question their presence.

'Come here,' he whispered.

Darcy did; there wasn't very far to go. They lay side by side, close but not touching, until with a hoarse groan he reached across with his good arm and drew her on top of him. His mouth reached hungrily for hers.

Darcy responded joyfully to the demands of his lips and thrusting tongue. It was intoxicating to have nothing to separate them any longer. Darcy wriggled to fully appreciate the sensation. His skin was warmer than hers; it was harder, and she discovered it had a deliciously smooth texture roughened by drifts of body hair that prickled against her breasts and thighs. Every detail delighted her and increased the pressure of excitement building inside her to detonation point.

'For a one-handed man,' she remarked a hundred or so gasps later, 'you manage pretty well.'

A savage grin split Reece's face as he looked into her flushed, aroused face. 'If you think that was good, wait until you get a taste of no hands.'

A confused frown drew Darcy's feathery brows together as she puzzled over his words, the meaning of which was brought crashing home to her seconds later.

Shock tensed her muscles for a split-second before she gave a languid sigh and relaxed. She moaned his name out loud and writhed restlessly as his tongue flickered lower over the soft curve of her abdomen. The excitement built to fever pitch as he continued his merciless ministrations.

The zip on the sleeping bag gave way as he brought her knees up and knelt between them, but Darcy didn't register the blast of cold air. The pleasure was so intense it bordered on pain; she cried out in protest but she cried out even louder when he stopped.

He kissed her, stilling her inarticulate protests.

He tasted and smelt of her and sex; it was a mind-shattering combination.

'I want you so badly!' she moaned, leaning her face into his neck.

'Then take me, sweetheart,' he urged throatily. 'Take me.'

Darcy lifted her head. 'I can. Can I…?' she gasped wonderingly. He whispered things in her ear that convinced her she could—she could do anything she wanted to.

Darcy stared down gloatingly at the magnificent man beneath her—his eyes were closed, his skin glistened with sweat. Her muscles tensed, she bore downwards. The cry of relief and triumph that was wrenched from her throat as she lowered herself upon him echoed around the room.

Reece's eyes snapped open. 'Oh, my God, sweetheart!' he groaned. 'You are…' A red mist danced before his eyes; he couldn't speak, he couldn't think, he could just thrust and thrust…

She rubbed her gritty-feeling eyes. Someone had carefully tucked the sleeping bag around her while she slept. Someone nothing. Her eyes went to the only other person in the room.

'Sleep well?' The fully clad figure bent over a portable keyboard didn't lift his dark head, but seemed to sense her wakefulness.

'Yes, thank you.' She tucked her nose below the covers. So this was that embarrassing morning-after feeling. 'What are you doing?'

'Sending a few e-mails.'

What sort of person sent e-mails at this time of the morning…? The sort of person you slept with last night—a *stranger*, her mental critic added, just in case she didn't feel bad enough already, a beautiful stranger.

'Right…' She cleared her throat. 'What time is it…?' she asked, more out of a desire to fill the yawning gap in their conversation than a genuine desire to know.

'Almost seven.'

'Seven!' she yelped, shooting upright. 'Oh, God!' she groaned, clasping her hands to her bare breasts.

Reece closed the lid of the laptop with a click and turned to face her. His gently ironic expression made her even more aware of the absurdity of displaying inhibitions the morning after the night before—especially when the night before was the one they'd shared!

'Is that a problem?'

'Dad and the boys will be up for breakfast,' she agonised.

'Can't they do *anything* without you to take charge?'

'Of course they can,' she responded, exasperated. 'And I don't "take charge".' Did she really strike him as a bossy, *organising* female? 'I just want things to be…' A frown puckered the smooth skin across her broad, seamless brow.

'The same?' he put in gently, drawing her startled gaze.

'I don't know what you mean.'

'Sure you do—you're trying to step into your mother's shoes. Has it ever occurred to you, Darcy, that maybe she wants her absence to be noticed…?'

A flicker of uncertainty made the soft corners of her mouth droop for a few tell-tale seconds before her expression hardened. 'You know nothing about it,' she blustered angrily. 'Mum isn't a frustrated housewife and she isn't menopausal.'

'Is that what the menfolk think…?'

Nick had put forward this theory but Darcy had soon put him right. 'Anyway, you're missing the point.'

He looked mildly perplexed. '*I* am…?'

'They'll wonder where I am.'

She watched his sensual lips twist. 'And you don't want to broadcast the fact you spent the night with me.'

The sad part was her reputation could probably survive intact. She'd learnt a long time ago that people didn't think of her and steamy sex in the same thought. She was doomed to be the eternal Mary Poppins figure. Which was pretty ironic when you had an almost ruined marriage on your conscience.

'Do you blame me?' she asked him scornfully. He didn't respond but a nerve along his jaw-line did some flexing. 'Relax,' she sighed disconsolately. 'Even if I did want to tell, nobody would believe me.'

Reece got to his feet and strolled towards her. 'Put this on—you look ridiculous.' He handed her her pyjama top.

His scornful contempt of her maidenly modesty was even more infuriating because she shared his opinion; even so, she couldn't bring herself to expose herself to the full glare of his scrutiny, which was, she reasoned gloomily, bound to be a whole lot more objective than it had been last night.

'If you're waiting for me to turn my back you'll be waiting a long, long time,' he drawled, taking up a grandstand seat on the packing case. He stretched out his long legs and casually crossed his booted feet at the ankle.

'You're no gentleman.'

He seemed to find her accusation amusing.

With an angry toss of her tousled hair she pulled the garment over her head.

It was a classic case of more haste, less speed. With her head halfway through the arm-hole she took a deep breath and told herself to calm down. So she didn't have the best boobs in the world—they were more than adequate…some might even say ample…what did it matter if he didn't grade them in the top ten per cent…? After all, they were only ships that had passed—and collided—in the night.

The rest of the manoeuvre was performed with a bit of belated dignity. She smoothed the fabric into place.

'I'm perfectly at ease with my body,' she declared defiantly. Why not just give him a list of your insecurities to peruse at his leisure and be done with it, you *idiot*!

'Oh, it shows, sweetheart, it shows,' came the bone-dry response.

Whilst his facial muscles didn't budge an inch, the sardonic amusement in his eyes said it all. Then suddenly he wasn't smiling any more and something was added to the atmosphere that hadn't been there a second before—something that made her heart-rate pick up tempo.

'Last night…' he began heavily.

Here was the point where he explained it had been great *but*... She jumped in to beat him to the punchline; no way could she endure the big brush-off she sensed was heading her way!

'Last night!' For some reason she found herself grinning in a manic kind of way across at him. 'Yes, mad wasn't it...?' She shrugged in a way that suggested that kind of madness came her way on a regular basis.

'Mad, bad...' his deep voice lovingly caressed each syllable and became diamond-hard as he continued '...mind-blowingly great sex...is that what you are trying to say?'

Darcy wasn't trying to say anything; she was trying to remember how to breathe! Not only did he sound as if he meant it, he looked it too. In fact, that mean, hungry look on his rampantly male features made her shudder inside and blush hotly on the outside—she wished she could have reversed the scenario; it would have shown less.

Now, here was something she hadn't bargained for. Was it a good or bad thing...?

With a rush she got to her feet and tugged the pyjama top down as far as it would go over her thighs.

'I'm glad you enjoyed yourself.' Of all the *moronic*... With a sigh of relief she located her clothes folded in a neat pile—Darcy retained a very definite memory of throwing them along with her inhibitions to the four winds the previous night. She found the thought of Reece retrieving and carefully folding her clothes somehow strangely unsettling.

'Did you?'

'You know I did,' she choked.

'I seem to recall your mentioning something to that effect,' he agreed.

Darcy choked some more.

'Why are you running away?' His languid tone suggested

casual curiosity rather than a driving desire to discover the reason.

Darcy zipped up her jeans, swearing softly as the zip snagged in the fabric of the pyjama trousers she had on underneath. 'That's rich coming from you!' she said, going into attack mode.

There was a tense silence.

'Meaning…?' Darcy had never heard that dangerous note in his voice before but she didn't doubt he used it often—and no doubt it had the desired effect of cowing the recipient. Well, not this time, mate…!

A mulish expression settled on her soft features as she planted her hands on her hips and laughed. 'You've got to be kidding…? You're holed up here; what's that if it's not running away?'

She watched the anger slowly fade from his eyes. 'Christmas. I'm running away from Christmas…'

A startled laugh was drawn from her. 'There's a lot of it around.' If all Mum was running away from was Christmas she'd be delighted—the complications arose if it was her life or, nasty thought, her family that had made her flee!

'Pardon…?'

Darcy shook her head. 'Nothing,' she prevaricated, her eyes sliding from his.

'Then why are you looking so shifty?' he wondered, displaying an unforgivable and highly worrying degree of perception.

'I've got that sort of face,' she snapped back bad-temperedly.

'You wouldn't make a poker player,' he agreed.

'I was just thinking.'

'Dare I ask what?'

'If you must know, I was thinking you don't strike me as the sort of man who runs away from anything. And even if you did, why on earth would you run away here…?' Her eyes did a quick, highly critical circuit of the room.

He shook his head and clicked his tongue. 'Don't let the Yorkshire Tourist Board hear you say that,' he chided.

'I meant this house.'

'Why not…?' he drawled.

'No electricity, I'm guessing poor plumbing…?' She began to tick off the reasons on her fingers.

'Diabolical,' he conceded ruefully. 'If you want the bathroom I'd wait until you get next door if I were you.'

'Thanks for the advice.' She refused to be sidetracked. 'You still haven't told me why.'

The imperious angle of his head made it seem as though he was looking down his masterful nose at her—Darcy didn't relish the sensation.

'Could that be because I don't think it's any of your business…?'

Darcy relished this sensation even less! She caught her breath angrily at the calculated rebuff.

'Well, that put me in my place, didn't it?'

A spasm of something close to regret flickered across Reece's features.

'Hold on.' He moved to intercept her before she reached the door. 'My friend's builders have been a little less than truthful with their reports to him,' he explained abruptly. 'I'd say they've fallen behind schedule by a couple of months. I was expecting something less…basic.'

'Then you're not staying?' *Of course he's not, dumbo.*

'I wasn't…'

Sure she must have misheard his soft response, Darcy raised her startled eyes to his face. 'What's changed?'

He was watching her with that infuriatingly enigmatic smile that told her absolutely nothing. 'I like the neighbours.'

Their eyes met and a great rush of sexual longing

crowded out sensible coherent thought. She never figured out how long she stood there staring at him like a drooling idiot.

Does he think all he has to do is click his fingers and I'll…? Why not, Darcy, girl, that's all he had to do last night! Her face flushed with mortification.

'Like the idea of sex on tap, you mean!'

His mouth tightened.

'Well, let me tell you, if you think last night was anything other than a one-off, think again!' she advised hotly.

'Does the idea of a relationship based on sex frighten you, Darcy?'

'No,' she told him candidly, 'it appalls me!'

'And excites you,' he interjected slyly.

'No such thing!' she blustered.

'Liar…you want me and we both know it.'

Darcy gave a hoarse, incredulous laugh—talk about Neanderthal. 'Why not just thump your chest and drag me off to your cave?'

Reece thought the general idea was sound, although he was thinking more along the lines of a nice hotel room with good plumbing and Room Service.

'It may not be a particularly politically correct thing to say, but—'

'May?' she squeaked. 'There's no "may" about it!'

'Tell me, do you regret last night happened? Do you regret we made love, Darcy?'

She lifted her chin, met his eyes scornfully, and opened her mouth. 'You bet I…' The blood drained dramatically from her face. 'I…*no*,' she admitted with the utmost reluctance—now would have been a good time to lie.

'As I was saying, from the first moment I saw you…'

Perhaps the significance of her confession was wasted on him…? Then again, perhaps this was wishful thinking on her part.

'The first moment you saw me you thought I was a boy. Is there something you're not telling me…?'

He eyed her with signs of irritation. 'So, not the *first*,' he gritted. 'We're not talking about *then*, we're talking about *now*.'

Darcy didn't want to talk about now—actually, she didn't want to talk about anything with this infuriating man who seemed to have the knack of making her say incriminating things.

'And now,' she announced coldly, 'I'm going home—or I would be if you'd shift yourself.' She looked pointedly past his shoulder at the door.

Reece immediately stepped to one side with a fluid grace that made her stomach muscles quiver; perversely she found herself reluctant to take the escape route offered.

Whilst she hovered indecisively he moved to her side. 'I'll walk you home.'

Darcy's eyes widened. 'You're joking—right?'

'Actually,' he confessed, 'I was hoping you'd let me have the use of your shower, or, better still, a long, hot bath.'

'My God, but you've got a nerve!' she gasped.

'I've also got several broken ribs, extensive bruising and a bust shoulder, but don't let that influence your decision.'

Despite herself, Darcy felt a smile forming. 'We're not a hotel!' she told him severely.

'Is that a no?'

Darcy's eyes narrowed. 'It should be.' He didn't look surprised by her capitulation, but then, why would he, when you've already proved you're a push-over in every sense of the word? 'If you say *anything* to my family about…you know what…'

'So, Darce…?'

'So what?' Darcy waved her secateurs in her brother's

face. 'If you're going to get in my way you might as well carry this lot.' She indicated the large pile of freshly cut holly at her feet.

'Me!'

My God, but men were hopeless. 'I suppose you'd just stand there and watch me shift the lot.' They'd certainly stand by and watch her decorate the house with boughs of festive greenery, not to mention decorate the enormous tree that by family tradition they collected from the local garden centre owned by her godparents.

'It's sharp.'

'It's holly, Nick; of course it's sharp.'

'This sweater cost me a fortune,' he grumbled, preceding her up the garden path. 'Where do you want it?' he asked when they eventually reached the house.

'Leave it in the porch. Feel like a cup of coffee?' she asked as her brother followed her into the house.

'I feel like some answers.'

Darcy, her expression suspicious, watched as he plucked a couple of stray glossy leaves from the fine rib of his sweater.

'About what?' she asked, trying not to sound defensive.

'About what you were doing with our neighbour. I thought you couldn't stand him.'

'I can't,' Darcy asserted stoutly. 'The man had a serious accident. What was I supposed to do—say he couldn't take a shower?' She turned away, crashing the cups and saucers. 'Did you say you wanted tea or coffee?'

'Neither. It would be when you bumped into him while you were walking the dogs that he asked to use our facilities, would it, Darce…?'

'Yes, that's right,' she agreed quickly, not turning around.

'Since when, little sister, did you take the dogs for a walk wearing your pyjamas?'

Darcy started and spilt the milk over the work surface.

'Language!' her brother reproached.

She shot him a withering glance and wiped her clammy palms on the seat of her jeans before she picked up the cup; the faint tremor in her fingers was barely noticeable—though eagle-eyed Nick had probably spotted it.

'Since when did you become Miss Marple?' She laughed lightly as she planted herself on a chair and raised the scalding drink to her lips. Playing it down was the best way to go…

'Since I looked into your room after I took the dogs for a walk around seven and found you weren't there.'

All the colour bar a small pink circle over either cheek fled Darcy's guilty face. 'What were you doing in my room?'

'Fetching you a cup of tea.'

It was typical of Nick to discover his considerate side at the worst possible moment. 'Oh…' What else could she say? She certainly wasn't going to volunteer any more information if she could help it!

'What is a guy like him with that sort of serious money doing hanging around someone like you?' Nick wondered suspiciously. 'No offence intended, Darce…' he added casually.

Darcy wondered what he'd say if she told him she took offence—serious offence. She was about to quiz her tactless sibling on the 'serious money' statement when his next comment distracted her.

'Has he followed you here, Darcy, is that it? I'm assuming you'd already met before yesterday.'

'Why on earth would you think that?' There was no way he could have picked anything up from her attitude when she'd brought Reece back earlier. She'd been very careful about that—so careful, in fact, that her behaviour had bordered on the catatonic, before she'd swiftly excused herself and nipped off to the church to do the flowers—it was Mum's turn on the rota; Adam would probably have a fit when he saw her efforts.

'I think that because I didn't think you were the sort of girl who would spend the night with a complete stranger.' If what he had said wasn't bad enough, Nick had to go and make it even worse by adding, 'Even if he is rich and powerful.'

For several moments Darcy didn't do anything, but when she finally lifted her eyes from the rim of her coffee-cup they were sparkling with anger.

'How dare you?'

Nick looked taken aback by the rancour in his sister's shaking voice. 'Come on, Darce, you must admit it was pretty sus…'

'I don't have to admit anything!' she said in a low, intense voice that throbbed with emotion. Carefully pushing her seat back, she rose to her feet. 'Not to you at least.' She ran her tongue over the bloodless outline of her pale lips. 'Just for the record, Nick, you're the biggest hypocrite I know.'

His eyes filled with concern, Nick rose to his feet. 'Darce, I didn't mean—'

Darcy cut him off with a flash of her narrowed eyes. 'Incidentally, I'll sleep with who the hell I like!' she yelled, sweeping from the room.

Her dramatic exit was ruined by the fact she narrowly avoided colliding with the solid bulk of Reece Erskine on her way out.

'Whoa there.' She'd have fallen rather than accept the arm he tried to offer her; it wasn't easy, as he was carrying a large wicker hamper balanced on the crook of his functioning elbow, and his solicitous action almost sent it to the floor.

'What are you doing here?' The tense, scratchy thing

didn't sound like her voice at all. Making a superhuman effort, she pulled herself together and stepped back away from his chest—and the temptation to lay her head on it. Even holding her breath, she could still smell the fresh male fragrance that emanated from his warm skin, so she gave up on what was not really a practical long-term solution to her problem to begin with.

'That's no way to greet a guy carrying gifts, Darce.'

Darcy hadn't even noticed the twins and Jack, who had entered the kitchen behind Reece—when he was around she didn't tend to notice much else.

'Cool!' Harry cried, holding up a large box of Belgian chocolates and adding them to the pile of luxury items he and his twin were extracting from the hamper they'd set down on the table.

Darcy glanced at the growing pile—there was no way he'd got that little lot from the village shop.

'This is mine,' Charlie crowed, discovering a bottle of champagne.

Clicking his tongue tolerantly, his father removed the bottle from his crestfallen son's hand. 'This is really very generous of you, Reece…'

'A small thank-you for everything you've done for me.'

'It really wasn't necessary,' Jack insisted.

'Dad, you're not going to give it back, are you?' Charlie asked in alarm.

'How did we raise two such avaricious little monsters…?' The twins exchanged rueful grins. 'What the boys are trying to say, Reece, is the gift is much appreciated. Can we offer you a drink—it looks like there's one on the go… Darcy…?'

'In case nobody noticed, I'm busy,' she responded shortly.

If her stepfather had looked annoyed by her unneighbourly response she could have coped, but no, he had to go and look hurt and guilty.

'I suppose,' he responded worriedly, 'we have let a lot of things fall on your shoulders.' He turned to Reece. 'It's just my wife usually…'

'I enjoy it, Dad,' Darcy interrupted hurriedly, hating the forlorn expression on her stepfather's face and despising herself for putting it there. 'Actually, I was just off to pick up the tree. Anyone like to come?' she enquired. She was predictably underwhelmed by the response. 'Right, I'll be off, then.'

'If you don't mind, I wouldn't mind coming along for the ride.'

Darcy spun around, horror etched on her pale features. 'You!'

'I'm getting a bit stir-crazy, unable to drive,' Reece explained glibly to the room in general.

'You'd be bored,' she said several shades too emphatically.

'I think it's an excellent idea,' Jack responded firmly, reproach in his eyes.

Nick spoke for the first time. 'I'm sure Darcy will enjoy having company.'

Darcy shot her treacherous narrow-minded brother a seething look from under the sweep of her lashes. 'There will be lashings of mud.' Nobody paid her any heed.

'Borrow some Wellingtons—the twins look about the same size as you.'

With a sigh Darcy subsided into a resentful silence whilst her eager family—with the notable exception of Nick—equipped their neighbour.

'You look awfully pale, Darcy.'

Thanks, bro, she thought as Nick's contribution to the conversation brought her a lot of highly undesirable attention.

'Yes, she does, doesn't she?' her stepfather agreed. 'Are you feeling all right?'

'Absolutely fine.'

'It's probably sleep deprivation,' Nick continued smoothly. 'She's not been sleeping too well.' He wasn't looking at his sister as he spoke but at the tall figure who stood beside her. The two men exchanged a long look.

'Is that right? You didn't say so, Darcy.'

'Lot on my mind, Dad…' she muttered. 'Holidays are always the same—it takes me the first week to wind down.'

'Darcy is a computer analyst,' her proud stepfather explained to Reece. 'She has a *very* responsible job.'

Darcy cringed. 'Give the man a break, Dad,' she laughed uncomfortably. 'I'm sure Mr Erskine doesn't want to know about my work.'

Nick, of course, couldn't resist stirring the pot. 'You mean, he doesn't already?'

'If you've got nothing better to do, Nick, you could take a look at the Christmas lights for me.' She felt a surge of satisfaction as her brother looked suitably horrified at the prospect. 'They don't seem to be working.'

'I think,' Nick announced hopefully, 'that it's time we bought some new ones.'

'You can't do that, Nick!' Charlie protested. 'We've had them for ever…'

'My point exactly,' Nick muttered. 'It's the same every year—they never work.'

'I remember the time the cat—that one that had no tail—' Harry began.

'Oscar,' his twin supplied.

Nick decided to inject a little reality into this trip down memory lane. '*I* remember the time they fused the electrics while Mum was cooking Christmas dinner…'

There was a collective subdued gasp of dismay and all eyes turned to Jack.

'Far be it from me to break with tradition,' Nick put in quickly. 'I'll fix the damned things.'

'You all seem pretty protective of your father,' Reece observed as he trailed Darcy outside.

'Stepfather, actually, but yes, I suppose we are.'

'Stepfather; that makes the twins your…?'

Darcy gave a resigned sigh. 'Jack adopted Nick and me when he married Mum—I was five. Not that it's any of your business.' She stood beside the Land Rover, jingling the keys. 'You can't *want* to come…' Please…please, let him say he doesn't. She always had been a hopeless optimist!

CHAPTER FIVE

'DID you have to bring this thing?' Reece scowled as the big dog, his paws planted on the back of the passenger seat, licked his face ecstatically.

'I wanted *him* to come,' Darcy, tight-lipped, pointedly replied. 'Sit down, Wally!' Reluctantly the big animal curled up on the back seat of her stepfather's Land Rover, his eyes reproachful.

Reece wiped the excess canine saliva off his neck with a pained grimace. 'A man could get to feel unwanted.'

'Not by Wally.' The dog's ears pricked up at the sound of his name. 'Or my family,' she reflected with a frustrated little snort. 'You've certainly weaseled your way into their affections,' she hissed nastily. 'It was a master stroke to appeal to the twins' stomachs.'

Reece, who wasn't really interested in the direct route to the twins' hearts, responded with a slightly distracted smile.

'I take it the way to your elder brother's heart is not through his stomach...'

'You noticed that, did you?' Darcy had not yet forgiven Nick. How dared he lecture her on morality, she fumed—the man who had had, much to his parents' dismay and her awe, an affair with a thirty-year-old divorcee when he was just seventeen?

'Let's just say I didn't feel warm and welcome when he looked at me,' Reece responded drily. His eyes narrowed. 'Is he giving you a hard time?' he wondered suspiciously.

'I don't give a damn what Nick thinks!'

'Yeah, I heard that bit.'

A deep tide of colour washed over her fair skin as she

worked out what he must have heard. 'Don't go reading anything into that. I was establishing a principle. Sex isn't a high priority for me.'

Darcy knew she was wasting her breath; the man obviously had her down as some sort of sex junkie—I could always refer him to Michael, she thought. He would set the record straight. Not that Michael had ever come right out and complained about her sex drive, or lack of it, but that was probably because the man had still had a wife at home to keep happy. From his point of view, the fact she hadn't made excessive demands had probably been a godsend!

'You got many other prospects lined up?'

'Has anyone ever told you you've got a very crude mouth, and a one-track mind?' He wasn't the only one, she thought, struggling hard to banish the image of his big, sexy body shifting beneath her…his skin glistening…the ripple of muscle… The heat travelled like a flash-flood up her neck and bathed her face. The empty feeling in the pit of her belly got emptier and achier.

Despite her determination to think of anything else but the man beside her, Darcy couldn't have stopped her eyes from furtively fluttering to the mouth she'd criticised if her life had depended on it. Perfection didn't seem too extravagant an adjective for that wide, mobile curve which intriguingly managed to combine both sensuality and control.

'Actually,' she mused, her voice husky, 'the new vicar did ask me to the Christmas dance.' She'd almost forgotten this unexpected event, which had occurred only this morning, but then she had other things on her mind. How her little sister would laugh if she ever discovered what a man-magnet the sister she despaired of had become.

'New vicar…' Reece didn't look as though he was taking the opposition seriously. 'I'm seeing tweed jackets, maybe a goatee—looks aren't everything, of course…'

'Actually, Adam played rugby for Oxford,' she was pleased to announce.

'In the Sixties…?'

'I'd say he's thirty…'

'Broken nose…?' Reece suggested hopefully.

Darcy's lips twitched. 'No, he was a back-row man. It was a toss-up between male modelling and the church,' she lied outrageously. Her expression sobered. 'Reece, are you?' she began.

'Am I what?'

'Nick said…' she began.

'Nick said what?' Reece thought he could guess.

'He said you were rich—super-rich, actually. Is that true?'

Reece didn't prevaricate. 'Yes.'

Deep down she'd always known he didn't live in the same world as she did. Darcy tried not to let her disappointment show; she'd been secretly hoping that Nick might have got it wrong. Now there was no point even dreaming this thing might be anything other than a one-night stand.

'I suppose you're famous too?' she accused bitterly.

She made it sound as though he'd been concealing the fact he was wanted by Interpol. Reece had never met a female who had reacted in quite this way to his social position and wealth before.

'Obviously not,' he drawled, amusement in his voice.

'Don't be offended,' she soothed absently. 'I don't read the financial pages.'

'But Nick does?'

'Hardly; he's a sports journalist.'

Reece laughed. 'I think you're being a bit severe; I knew a sports writer once who had read a book.'

Darcy couldn't summon the necessary smile to respond

to his raillery. 'Are you involved in property development? Is that why you came to the Hall?'

'My company is involved in property development,' Reece agreed, not mentioning that this property development didn't include small country houses being renovated on a shoestring.

It did involve a string of brand-new hotels in various capitals of the world which the leisure arm of his empire now ran. A good many office complexes and several sports stadiums which had popped up all over Europe had also begun their existence on a drawing board in the Erskine Building—he didn't mention this either.

'Then you're some sort of property developer…?' she prodded.

'That was one of the areas we've diversified into during the last few years.'

'We?'

'Well, it's not a one-man show; my sister Kate is heavily involved in the running of the hotel chain, and my cousin Declan has just joined us. My kid brother has just finished his stint at Harvard, so hopefully he'll—'

'You told me you didn't have a family!' Darcy twitched her rear-view mirror and saw an almost comical grimace of dismay register on his drop-dead gorgeous features.

'I did…?' he echoed evasively.

'Yes, you did.'

'They're a lovely bunch but a bit…overwhelming *en masse*—like at Christmas time. Don't you ever wish you were an only child…?'

The encounter with Nick still fresh in her mind, Darcy found herself nodding. 'When I'm around Nick, yes, I do.'

'The guy's only trying to protect you.' Reece had a sister of his own, and a real headache she was too.

Darcy could hardly believe her ears—Reece, defending Nick of all people! 'This male bonding is all very sweet but have you forgotten it's you he wants to protect me from?' she reminded him.

'I'd not forgotten. I have this nasty feeling when he gets me alone he's going to ask me what my intentions are.'

Did he really expect her to appreciate the humour of this remark? 'He already knows. That's the problem.'

She sensed his looking at her, and couldn't stop herself taking her eyes off the road for a split-second…he was pushing an unruly hank of glossy almost black hair from his eyes. Did he always have to look so damned pleased with himself? she wondered, resenting the way just looking at him sent her temperature rocketing.

Reece would have been astonished if he'd been privy to her thoughts. He had rarely felt less complacent in his life; things were happening to him that he didn't want or need—his eyes were drawn to the shell-like shape of her ear—cancel 'didn't need'. Every time he looked at this woman he *needed* with a capital N.

'Perhaps he could tell me,' he muttered under his breath.

'Pardon?'

She wanted to know; well, he'd tell her! 'I can't look at your ear without wanting to whisper in it. I can't look at your mouth—'

'Stop!' Darcy yelled, her stressed heart pumping out adrenalin like a pneumatic drill. 'If you say things like that I'm likely to crash the car.'

'In that case, wouldn't it be far safer if you parked somewhere? Somewhere quiet and secluded would be good.' From what he'd seen, that shouldn't be too difficult—they'd barely passed another car.

Darcy broke out in a cold sweat. 'You can't say things like that to me!' She could hardly hear herself speak above the frantic clamour of her heart.

Reece sighed. 'I can't *not* say things like that to you. Do you think it's possible they've put something in the water...?'

'I think it's possible you've got nothing better to do than harass me,' she responded weakly in a strangulated version of her own deep, husky voice.

'Actually, I brought a heap of paperwork with me.'

'I'm flattered no end.'

'Do your boyfriends always have to work so hard?'

She could have said What boyfriends? but she didn't want to reveal the disgraceful lack of sexual encounters in her work-orientated life. 'You're not a boy or my friend.'

'I'm your lover.'

This man was the master of the one-liners; there was no doubt about it. Darcy dabbed the beads of sweat from the full outline of her upper lip with the tip of her tongue and tried to coax her respirations into a more manageable rate.

'You're my one-night stand,' she bit back coldly. He would never know that this admission hurt her more than it did him. 'Listen, I can see why you might think I'm up for...that I might want you to...' Darcy's voice dropped to an agonised whisper. 'You know what I mean.' Still he didn't respond. 'Last night wasn't me...'

Even though her eyes remained rigidly fixed on the road, she could feel his eyes travelling over her body, her skin prickling in response to the unseen scrutiny.

'I have to dispute that.'

The low rasp of his voice was like a caress, and she could picture his slow, sensual smile in her head. She ground her teeth in frustration.

'I don't normally act like that,' she insisted.

'Then last night was special...?'

'Last night was mad, a mistake!' she yelled. 'I'm not passing judgement on people that do act like that, but it's just not me.'

'I think it is you.'

'Haven't you heard a thing I've said?' she asked shrilly.

'You've made a lot of noise but you haven't come right out and said no.'

She gave a contemptuous laugh. 'And I'm supposed to believe that's all it takes…?'

'Believe it or not, it's true.'

You could have taken a chainsaw to the tension in the air.

'Will you fasten your seat belt?'

Reece smiled, but didn't push his advantage. 'It hurts the bust ribs,' he explained mildly.

So would being thrown through the windscreen. 'Don't be such a sissy!' she admonished sternly.

'You're the boss.'

If only, she thought wistfully. I should have said no—why didn't I say it…? 'If the word "mouth" crosses your lips once more I'll make you walk back,' she warned him sternly. Darcy had no intention of becoming a rich man's plaything—no matter how tempting the notion was.

'Last night—'

Darcy cut him off. 'That too.'

'I have a very extensive vocabulary, Darcy.'

'And I have a very low tolerance level.' Her angry sneer morphed into a weak scowl. 'Why the hell did you come here?' If he hadn't been doing so she'd never have met him and her life would have been a lot simpler.

'Maybe I got tired of well-meaning people trying to rehabilitate me.'

Darcy puzzled over his obscure reply. 'I don't understand.'

'That's the way I'd like to keep it for the moment.'

There was only a handful of people in the garden centre, but Reece suspected they'd have come in for personal attention even if the place had been packed out. As if he'd been expecting them, the guy Reece assumed ran the place appeared as soon as they drew up. He greeted Darcy warmly and enfolded her in a bear-like hug. When she emerged she reluctantly acknowledged his presence.

'This is Richard Stenning, my godfather. Uncle Rick, this is Reece, and, before you say anything, he's *not* my boyfriend.'

'But I'm working on it.'

Both men seemed to find this crack amusing; Darcy didn't.

'I was thinking between six feet and six feet six...?' she said briskly, eyeing up the swathes of green pine.

'I'm six four and a half actually.'

'Not you, *stupid*, the tree.'

The older man looked at the bickering couple with a benevolent smile. 'Come along this way, Darcy, I think I've got just what you want.'

Darcy doubted this very much unless he had a supply of six-foot-four-and-a-half males with fascinating green eyes, black hair and sex appeal that went off the scale! Despite this, she stomped obediently after him.

Despite Reece's unhelpful contributions, she eventually selected one that was neither too bushy nor too straggly and didn't have any bare bits. The tree was bagged in a net and installed in the back of the Land Rover beside Wally.

'You'll have a mince pie, of course?'

Reece bent downwards to enquire in her ear, 'Is this another family tradition?'

Darcy ignored him and the tantalising male scent of him that teased her receptive nostrils—she was partially successful.

'Wouldn't miss it for the world,' she agreed, following their host into the shop area, which was dripping with both tasteful and gaudy Christmas decorations—not the place for a man who was trying to avoid Christmas, although Reece seemed to be taking the festive surroundings in his stride. 'But no sherry for me,' she added hastily, with an expression of regret, 'I'm driving.'

'But you'll have some, Mr Erskine?'

'Reece. Yes, I'd love some.'

Darcy was watching from under the protective sweep of her lashes, so she had the satisfaction of seeing his eyes widen in shock as he took a robust bite from his innocent-looking pie. Her lips twitched; she was far more tentative in her approach.

'Delicious as usual,' she mumbled, chewing away valiantly; Uncle Rick must have a stomach of cast iron, she decided, watching him munch his way through two for her one. The problem with Aunty Grace's mince pies was that they looked totally delicious and had the consistency of concrete. 'Aunty Grace has surpassed herself this year.'

'Delicious,' she heard Reece agree faintly after he very visibly swallowed.

'Would you like another, Reece?'

Reece patted his stomach. 'Love to, but I don't want to take the edge off my appetite—I'm taking Darcy to lunch,' he explained glibly.

'First I've heard about it.'

'It was meant to be a surprise, darling.' He glanced at the steel-banded watch on his wrist. 'Talking of which, we should be making a move—I've booked a table for twelve.'

'Where would that be...*darling*?' she wondered innocently. The man was entirely too slick.

'Why, where else but your favourite, *daaarling*?' Reece drawled smoothly.

'Twelve...? You'd better get a move-on, Darcy; it'll take you twenty minutes to get to the Bull's Head. You give my best to the family.'

Darcy bent forward and kissed the older man's cheek. 'I will, Uncle Rick. Why, Reece!' she exclaimed, picking up the glass carefully secreted behind a potted palm. 'You've forgotten your sherry,' she reminded him spitefully.

'So I have.' He met her eyes and, nostrils flared, tipped back the glass, downing the contents in one gulp—like taking nasty medicine, she thought, stifling the urge to giggle.

'Was that a test, or an initiation ceremony?' he muttered under his breath as they walked together back to the Land Rover.

If it had been he'd have passed with flying colours. 'Uncle Rick only hands out the mince pies and sherry to valued friends and customers.'

'I'm surprised he still has any.'

'Shut up,' she hissed, waving through the window. 'He'll hear you.'

'What was that I just drank?'

'Sherry.'

'I've tasted sherry, sweetheart, and that wasn't it.'

Darcy, who had sampled the sweet, syrupy concoction in the past, had some sympathy with his view. 'It's probably safer to call it fortified wine,' she conceded.

'How about we head for the Bull's Head, your favourite watering hole?' he reminded her drily.

'How about I drop you at the nearest bus station? Oh, sorry, I forgot I'm talking to limo man.'

'Helicopters are my preferred mode of transport. Do you realise that nearly all our conversations have taken place while you're at the wheel of a car—?'

'Is there anything wrong with my driving?' she asked belligerently.

'Not a thing—when you're looking at the road. It would make a nice change to be able to have a conversation that doesn't prohibit the odd physical gesture.'

Darcy swallowed nervously and decided it would be safer to never relinquish her place at the wheel. 'Your problem,' she announced scornfully, 'is you think I'll agree to anything if you kiss me.'

'From where I'm sitting that's a revelation not a problem.'

It was one revelation too many for Darcy; she couldn't concentrate on the road when her mind was full of forbidden images. The battle of words, at times undeniably stimulating, had lost all appeal. With a muffled plea for heavenly intervention she brought the Land Rover to an abrupt halt on the grassy verge. Without even bothering to switch off the engine, she leapt from the driver's seat.

Reece switched off the engine and pocketed the keys before following her.

Darcy, who was hunched over, her hands braced against her thighs, turned her head to look at him.

'Go away!' she pleaded hoarsely. She didn't actually hold out much hope of his doing as she requested.

'Are you all right?'

'Very obviously not.' She took another deep breath and slowly straightened up. She brushed a few stray strands of hair from her face; it was an intensely weary gesture. 'If you must know, I couldn't stand being in that car with you any longer.' She was past caring what he thought.

Reece didn't seem to take offence in her anguished observation. 'It's pretty intense, isn't it?' he commiserated.

Darcy's brows drew into a suspicious line above her wide, startled eyes. 'Are you saying that *you*...?' She moved her head in a scornful negative gesture, rejecting the idea that Reece could be similarly affected by her proximity.

'I can't stop thinking about last night or wanting it to happen again.' His tone might have been matter-of-fact bordering on rudely abrupt, but the lick of flames in his deepset eyes was not!

Darcy was shaking so hard she had to fold her arms tight

across her middle to hide the tremors. In the process she unwittingly drew attention to her full, heaving bosom. 'That was sex.'

'That was *exceptional* sex,' Reece contradicted firmly. 'A relationship has to start somewhere.'

Darcy looked at him blankly. 'Relationship…? You don't want a relationship.'

'How do you know what I want?' he demanded.

'Well, do you?'

'Maybe not. Well, actually, no, I don't want a relationship. I don't want to be celibate either.'

He didn't even have the guts to look her in the eye when he said it, she thought wrathfully. The perversity of the average male was simply breathtaking. But it had shut up the voice in her head, the one recklessly shrieking 'Go for it! Go for it!', and a good thing too, she decided glumly.

'The only thing I know for sure I want is you.'

She couldn't legitimately complain about eye-contact now—an earthquake couldn't have broken the grip his dark-lashed eyes had on her. The air escaped her lungs in one long, sibilant hiss; her eyes, huge in her pale face, were glued to his face. Her thoughts were in total chaos. You can't let yourself be seduced by someone saying he wants you—even if that someone is Reece Erskine, she told herself angrily.

'Naturally I'm flattered,' she drawled, giving a scornful, unnatural little laugh that implied just the opposite.

His jaw tightened. 'I'm not trying to flatter you.' Reece, who prided himself on self-control, discovered he couldn't take his eyes from the lush curve of her lovely lips, even though the looking caused the distant buzzing in his head to increase significantly.

'What are you trying to do, then?' Other than drive me out of my mind, that is…? It just didn't seem possible for a man to walk into her life and turn everything upside-down. 'You may be in the mood for some sort of holiday romance, but I simply don't have the time, energy or inclination.' Well, the first two at least were true.

'I thought you were on holiday too.'

Some holiday! 'My mum's gone walkabout, my stepfather, who I happen to be crazy about, needs constant reassurance, several hundred members of the family are likely to descend on us at any second and I can't even bake a mince pie, let alone feed and entertain them!' Stupidly it was the last deficiency that made her eyes fill with tears.

Reece moved towards her and she ached to throw herself into his arms. With a stiff little gesture that shrieked rejection she swayed backwards; it stopped Reece in his tracks.

'Are you trying to tell me this isn't a good time for us?' There was no smile to match the flippancy of his tone.

Darcy wanted to cry from sheer frustration, but she didn't have the luxury. As right as it felt to have his arms close around her, she knew it was all an illusion created by her overactive hormones. If she had been after casual sex she wouldn't have looked any further than this man: he fulfilled every criteria for the role.

The problem was she couldn't be that casual about sex, and when she got involved serious disaster usually followed—she was thinking about the rat Michael here, the one who had forgotten to mention his wife and children. His wife with kids in tow landing up on her doorstep pleading with Darcy not to take her husband away was one of her least favourite memories. Just recalling Michael's defence made her blood boil— 'I wanted to tell you, Darce, but I didn't want to hurt you'.

'There is no us!'

'There could be if you let it happen.'

And letting it happen would be so easy. Darcy sighed; his voice had a dangerously mesmeric quality…it was so hypnotic and attractive, in fact, that a person was inclined to forget just how outrageous the sentences formed by these perfect lips were.

'You're really worried about your mother, aren't you…?'

This observation brought her back to reality with a resounding thump.

'Am I supposed to believe you care about what I'm worried about?' she sneered, eyeing him with open contempt. 'The only thing you care about as far as I can see is getting me back into your bed!'

It was true, but that didn't alter the fact her words made him mad as hell. The flare of something close to fear in her eyes made him realise that his feelings must have been reflected on his face, so he made a conscious effort to control his anger.

'Listen, sweetheart,' he said after he'd counted to ten a couple of times, 'I've absolutely no idea if this thing is going to run its course in a matter of days, weeks or months but I think for both our sakes we should find out. If we don't we'll always wonder…' He paused long enough for her to appreciate the truth of what he was saying. 'I know you've some sort of guilt trip about sleeping with me last night, but it happened and I don't see much point beating yourself up over it.'

'Maybe I wouldn't if you didn't keep throwing it back in my face. Just for the record, I'm not…easy!'

'Just for the record,' he retorted drily, 'I don't think you're *easy*…anything but, as a matter of fact,' he added in a wry aside. 'This isn't the sort of attraction you can pretend isn't there, Darcy.'

That was true.

'I may want to get you into bed,' he continued with a candour that made her mouth grow dry and started up the distressing palpitations once more, 'but it doesn't mean we can't communicate outside the bedroom.' Darcy had no way of knowing how extraordinary this statement was coming from Reece Erskine, and Reece wasn't about to tell her—the truth was, it made him uneasy to acknowledge it. 'You're obviously worried about your mother and I thought it might help to talk to someone not personally involved. I may be shallow but I'm not totally insensitive.'

He sounded genuine. She searched his face—he looked genuine. 'I was only talking to her the day before; she didn't give a clue anything was wrong.' Her fingers clenched tightly.

'And you think you've done something?'

'Not me personally maybe—but us, the family. Why else would she walk out like this just before Christmas? She's made sure we can't contact her…' She gnawed away silently on her lower lip as she puzzled over the bizarre, bewildering behaviour of her parent.

'It's possible this is *her* problem.'

Darcy regarded him with disdain. 'Families are there to help you with your problems; you don't shut them out when you most need them.' An expression she didn't understand flickered across his handsome face. 'It's not at all like her—she's so *responsible*. Poor Jack is convinced it's something he's done.'

'But you don't think so.'

Darcy shook her head jerkily; now she'd started to talk it was hard to stop. 'Why couldn't she talk to us…?' she wondered unhappily.

'I expect you'll be able to ask her yourself when she comes home.'

In front of Jack and even her brothers she had to act optimistic and upbeat, and it was a relief almost to stop being so damned cheerful. 'Whenever that might be.'

'You've no idea at all how long she's likely to be away?'

Despondently Darcy shook her head. 'I'm really trying hard to make everything the same as it usually is…' It seemed important somehow not to let things slip, to keep a sense of continuity.

'And driving yourself into an early grave in the process,' he observed disapprovingly. 'The secret of a successful manager is delegation, Darcy.' She looked so transparently touched by his comment that he felt impelled to add, 'You ought to try it; you might even find you've got time for a personal life, and, as you already know, I have a vested interest in that.'

She stared wonderingly up into his face. It sounded as if he was saying he wanted to be part of her personal life, which didn't fit with what he had said about not wanting a relationship—in fact, it seemed to directly contradict it. The warmth in his eyes made her lose track for a few moments. 'How would I go about doing that?'

'You really want to know?'

Darcy gave a rueful smile. 'I wouldn't have asked otherwise.'

'Make a list of things you need to do and halve it.' She opened her mouth to protest but he didn't give her the opportunity. 'Divide the remaining tasks amongst the others. And don't tell me you can't give orders because I've been on the receiving end. Actually,' he admitted, his firm tone gentling, 'I quite liked it. Some of the time I quite like you...'

Darcy gulped. 'And the rest...?' she prompted huskily.

'I want to throttle you.'

'Which is it now?'

'Neither. It's been a hell of a long time since I wanted to wake up beside someone.'

'You're not trying to tell me you're celibate?'

'No, I'm not,' he agreed tersely. 'Sex is one form of recreation that I've made a point of including in my schedule,' he explained casually.

There was an appalled silence.

'That sounds pretty cold-blooded.' If she'd any sense she'd get back into the Land Rover and drive away. Darcy knew she wouldn't—she *couldn't.*

'It's an accusation that has been levelled at me before.'

'You want to kiss me.' It was a statement, not a question—it was the sort of statement that a girl who didn't want to be kissed didn't make.

'For starters,' he growled.

'Then for God's sake,' she pleaded in an agonised whisper, '*Do it!*'

My God, but the man could move fast with the right motivation. She barely had time to draw breath let alone change her mind before his mouth was hard on hers, and his tongue began to make some electrifying exploratory forays into the warm, moist interior.

The sheer pleasure of his touch as his fingers slid surely under the woollen jumper she wore made her whimper and sag, weak-kneed, against him. His hand worked its way smoothly up the slender curve of her back. Darcy grabbed for support and then remembered his injuries.

'I forgot.'

Reece's mouth came crashing back down on hers and stole away the rest of her words.

Eyes closed, she gave a long, blissful sigh when his head eventually lifted. 'I've hurt you.' She made an agitated effort to pull back, but he had other ideas.

'If I can't cope I'll tell you,' he breathed into her mouth.

'I don't think I can cope with much more of this!' she breathed back, touching her tongue to the fleshy inner part of his upper lip. She shuddered—they both did.

'Cope with what?'

Darcy laid her hand flat against his chest, feeling his heart beat through the layers of clothing. She'd known him for less than forty-eight hours and already he'd taken over her thoughts. If she had any sense she'd call it a day now before things got any worse.

'Cope with...*wanting*.' She put all the aching longing in the one word.

What was happening to her—where had this wilful recklessness come from? After Michael she'd been cautious—pathologically so, Jennifer had said. Would Jennifer approve of the new Darcy? The one who saw the flare of fierce possession in his eyes and felt the heat melt her bones and didn't even once contemplate running for cover? Hell, what did it matter? She needed action not analysis, and she needed Reece.

'Does that mean you've stopped trying to push me away?'

'I don't recall doing much pushing.' Grabbing, that was another matter.

'Why fight...?'

'My thought exactly.'

'It'll burn itself out soon enough.' Wasn't that the way with hot things? 'And I can get back to normal.'

Though his own thoughts had been running much along the same lines, Reece found that her sentiments filled him with a sense of discontent. He was perfectly aware that for a man who had a policy of never spending the entire night with a woman this was a pretty perverse response. Knowing it made no sense didn't lessen the gut feeling.

'And normal is...?' He slid his thumb down the soft curve of her cheek.

There was danger and raw, unrefined charisma in his smile. Without waiting for her to reply, he dipped his head and parted her lips with masterful ease.

'This normal...?' His tongue stabbed and she moaned low in her throat and pressed herself tight against his hips. She wondered vaguely if he was permanently aroused—not that she had any major objections if this should be the case. 'Or this…?' He withdrew.

Darcy gave a whimper of protest as he lifted his head.

'I preferred the first,' she admitted huskily.

'That being the case, perhaps we should…' He dangled the Land Rover keys in front of her. 'Can you drive…?'

Darcy nodded her head vigorously. So fierce was her need that if flying had been the only way to get into bed with him she'd have sprouted wings!

CHAPTER SIX

DURING the afternoon there had been several flurries of snow, and by the time Darcy got back home complete with the Christmas tree and a slightly guilty conscience a little of the powdery whiteness had begun to stick to the damp ground.

She stamped her feet to loosen the snow on her boots and lifted the old-fashioned iron latch on the kitchen door, hoping as she did so that there was nobody about; it wasn't that she intended to be *furtive*, exactly. 'Furtive' implied she had something to hide or be ashamed of, and, whilst Darcy acknowledged she was deeply confused and wildly exhilarated by what had happened to her, shame didn't feature at all. It was just that there were some things you couldn't share with your family, no matter how close you were, and Darcy didn't see much point in drawing unnecessary attention to her extended absence.

'Where have you been?'

So much for subterfuge.

Her entire family minus only one important member were seated around the long farmhouse table, but that absence brought an aching lump to her throat—if there was ever a time she'd needed her mum it was now. Darcy swallowed; she didn't need this, not when her mind was still full of the passionate coupling which had just taken place next door. She felt as if the evidence of her abandoned behaviour was written all over her face.

'Clare, you're home.' If Clare noticed her half-sister's greeting was lacking a certain warmth she didn't show it.

'Finally,' Nick contributed drily. 'Had trouble choosing the right tree, did you?' he wondered guilelessly.

Unexpectedly it was Clare who came to her rescue. 'Never mind about that, Nick.'

I'll second that, Darcy thought, pulling off her mittens. 'Good journey, Clare?'

'In case you hadn't noticed, it's snowing.' Clare's expression suggested that Darcy was in some way to blame for this.

I didn't notice because I've spent the afternoon making wild, passionate love to a gorgeous man. How, Darcy wondered, would that explanation go down…?

Clare shook back her rippling waist-length mane of hair and looked impatient. Like her half-sister, she was blonde and blue-eyed, but that was where the resemblance ended.

'I arrive to find that my mother…' she choked tearfully.

'She's ours too.'

'Shut up, Harry! Why didn't anyone tell me what was happening?'

'We didn't want to upset you, darling,' Jack soothed.

Nobody, Darcy reflected, feeling a twitch of resentment, ever wanted to upset Clare.

'Well, I'm upset now.' Clare sniffed.

'Did you remember to pick up the order from the farm, Nick?' Darcy asked, shaking her hair free of a few stray snowflakes, which were rapidly melting in the warm room. She hung her damp coat on the peg behind the door.

'How can you act as if nothing has happened?' Clare tearfully accused Darcy.

The implication that she didn't give a damn made Darcy turn angrily on her sister. 'What do you expect me to do, Clare?' she snapped. 'Mum's a grown woman; we can't bring her back against her will. We just have to wait.' Patience never had been one of her younger sister's most obvious qualities—when Clare wanted something she wanted it *now*, and more often than not she got it! 'Sitting about whining isn't going to help anyone!'

There was an almost comical look of shock on Clare's face as she recoiled from her sister's anger—Darcy was a bit surprised herself, as she rarely raised her voice to her sister. Instantly she regretted her outburst, not to mention her ungenerous thoughts. Clare could be thoughtless and selfish, but her kid sister could also be generous and loving, and not nearly as hard-bitten as she liked to make out.

There was a scraping sound as the younger girl rose gracefully to her feet. Darcy was happy being herself, but she wouldn't have been human if she hadn't felt the occasional touch of wistful envy when she looked at her spectacularly beautiful sister. Occasionally on bad days, when her hair was particularly unruly and the bathroom scales told her things she'd rather not know, she couldn't help but think that it would be nice if—just once—someone took notice of *her* when she walked into a room beside her gorgeous sister.

Seeing her sister stand there, tall, willowy and with a face and figure that would have stood out as exceptional on any catwalk, Darcy knew this was only going to happen in her wildest dreams.

Clare had no qualms about using her looks when it suited her, but she'd never had any intention of making her living out of them. Thanks to a big injection of capital from her parents, her dreams of becoming a fashion designer were well on the way to becoming a reality. She'd started her own business straight from art college and she had ambitious plans for her fashion label.

'We're all missing her, Clare,' Darcy said quietly. From the corner of her eye, she saw Harry reach across and hug his dad and the emotional lump in her throat ached.

'I know,' Clare admitted huskily. 'Sorry. Is the other thing true, or is Nick winding me up…?'

'Is what true...?' Darcy responded cagily. What had Nick the wind-up artiste been saying this time? she wondered, shooting her brother a suspicious glance. She didn't have to wait long to find out.

'Nick says that *Reece Erskine*...' Clare murmured the name in a dreamy, reverential way that made Darcy stiffen in alarm '...is staying next door—which is very obviously impossible,' she added quickly. 'I suppose he *is* having me on...?' Despite her conviction that this was a wind-up, there was a gleam of hope in her eyes as she appealed to her big sister.

'Yes, he is staying next door,' Darcy disclosed reluctantly. She watched her sister go pale with excitement.

'Why would...?' Clare began. 'No, it doesn't matter. Let me think... This is too marvellous...!'

Darcy thought so, but she had mixed feelings—no, actually, they weren't mixed at all; she didn't like the idea of Clare thinking Reece's proximity was marvellous one little bit.

'It is?'

'Of course it is, silly!' Clare exclaimed. 'Did you invite him for dinner, Darce...?' Her lovely face creased with annoyance. 'Of course you didn't,' she predicted critically. Her exasperation increased as the jerky little movement of Darcy's head confirmed her suspicions. 'Honestly, Darcy! What were you thinking of?'

Reece's tongue sliding smoothly skilful over her stomach...his burning eyes devouring her, the tiny quivering contractions that tightened her belly as she was overwhelmed by an almost paralysing desire to have him deep inside her.

'Are you listening to me, Darcy?'

The shrill, indignant sound of her sister's voice broke through the sensual thrall of her recollections. Darcy was appalled and slightly scared by her lack of self-control.

Sweat trickled damply down her stiff spine, and her cheeks felt as if they were on fire.

'I haven't got the time to have a dinner party, Clare,' she told her sister gruffly.

Her words fell on selectively deaf ears.

'Better still!' Clare, the bit firmly between her pearly teeth, enthused excitedly, 'We could invite him to stay. Yes, why not…? According to Dad, the Hall is not fit for human habitation.' She clapped her hands, her eyes glowing with enthusiasm. 'Yes, that would be perfect! Is anyone going to answer that?' she exclaimed, irritated by the persistent ring of the phone in the hallway.

Jack rose from his chair and put his hand on Darcy's shoulder. 'I'll go.'

'Perfect for what?' asked Charlie, who was growing bored with the subject, when his father had left the room. 'I don't see what's so great about the guy next door. You haven't even met him.'

Clare turned to her young brother, her expression one of supreme scorn for his ignorance.

'Don't you know anything…? He's one of the richest men in the country—he inherited a fortune from his grandfather and he's doubled it, or trebled it, whatever.' With a graceful flick of her wrist Clare dismissed the odd million or ten.

'That would explain the Merc in the shed,' Harry remarked thoughtfully to his brother.

'Have you two been spying?' Darcy exclaimed in a horrified tone.

'No harm done, Darce,' Harry soothed. 'Nobody was around. We saw some guys delivering this bed, though—gigantic thing it was, so he must be thinking about staying.'

Darcy, who knew all about the bed, tried to blend in with the furniture. If anyone looked at her now they would know—they'd just *know*…!

'Is he as good-looking as he looks in the photos I've seen of him?'

'I thought it was his money you were interested in.' Harry received an annoyed glare for his insensitive comment. 'I suppose you think he's going to take one look at you and propose you share his bed and bank account,' he sniggered.

'It has been known,' Clare confirmed calmly.

The awful part was that her sister's complacence was perfectly understandable—Darcy could see it all: Reece blinded by Clare's beauty, wondering what he'd ever seen in the dowdy little sister with the funny nose. Why hadn't she foreseen this? she wondered bitterly.

If the loud, realistic gagging noises Harry made as he headed for the door dragging his twin with him were anything to go by, her comment made him feel sick too.

Charlie seemed perfectly willing to follow his twin but he couldn't resist a taunting parting shot. 'What makes you think he's not already got a girlfriend or a wife even…?'

'Those boys get worse!' Clare exclaimed angrily as the door slammed behind them. 'He hasn't, has he, Darce?' she added worriedly.

'How should I know?' Helping her sister seduce her own lover was above and beyond the call of sisterly duty.

'Well, you have seen more of him than everyone else.'

'Something gone down the wrong way, Darce?' Nick asked solicitously.

'Do you want a drink of water?' Clare asked

Darcy wiped the moisture from the corner of her eye. 'I'm fine,' she protested hoarsely. The image in her mind of Reece's powerful body slick with sweat, his powerful thighs quivering with need and power, made it difficult for her to formulate a suitable reply. 'He didn't discuss his personal life with me, Clare.'

The indentation between her brows deepened as it struck

her forcibly just how adept he'd been at distracting her when their conversation had begun to touch on personal areas, but then his methods of distraction were in a class of their own. Married men acted like that...what if he'd been lying all along...? Clammy perspiration broke out along her brow as her tummy tied itself in knots of apprehension.

Darcy took a deep breath and firmly pushed aside her fears; this was her own insecurity at work. Reece wasn't the type to resort to subterfuge—let's face it, she thought, he doesn't need to! He'd been upfront enough—he wanted sex and nothing more.

'I can't believe you wasted all that time.'

'I wouldn't call it wasted exactly.' The way she recalled it, there hadn't been a second they hadn't filled with touching or tasting or *taking*... Darcy was confused on any number of matters but one thing was clear to her—she was glad they'd been lovers. She would always treasure the memory and no matter what the outcome that much at least wouldn't change.

'Oh, you're hopeless, Darcy!'

Hopelessly in love. Darcy felt as though a large fist had landed a direct hit on her solar plexus. Suddenly the missing pieces of the emotional jigsaw fell into place. Her mouth opened and closed several times as she gasped for air like a land-locked fish. If anyone had noticed her condition they would no doubt not have considered it attractive—but nobody did.

'I have made some enquiries...'

Clare squealed and gave her older brother her immediate approving attention. 'Why, you clever old thing, you. And...?'

'He's a widower.'

'Excellent!' Clare exclaimed gleefully; unlike Darcy, she didn't detect any undercurrent in Nick's words.

'Clare!' Darcy exclaimed, unable to hide her shocked disapproval.

'There's no more edifying sight,' Nick drawled to nobody in particular, 'than a woman in full pursuit.'

'I thought hunting was your favourite pastime, Nick…? But, silly me, you're a man, so that makes it all right, doesn't it?' Darcy heard herself perversely defending her sister.

Nick grinned. 'Sexist down to my cotton socks,' he conceded good-naturedly. 'I can't help myself any more than you can help yourself being scrupulously fair, Darce—even when it's not in your best interests,' he added in an amused but not unsympathetic undertone.

'Thank you, Darce. There's no need for either of you to look like that,' Clare insisted with a moody little pout. 'It's just such an excellent opportunity for me. It's not as if I'm going to marry him or anything.' A naughty grin flickered across her face. 'Unless, of course, the opportunity arises,' she added with a husky laugh. She shrugged when neither of her siblings showed any appreciation of her joke. 'Can you imagine how much free publicity I'd get being seen with Reece Erskine? It could really be the break I've been waiting for. It's perfectly legitimate,' she announced, a shade of defiance entering her voice.

Darcy couldn't help but wonder if her sister actually believed that. 'Dad would go spare if he could hear you.'

'Well, he can't, can he?' Clare pointed out unrepentantly. 'And what he doesn't know won't harm him—unless you tell him…'

'I can see it would put the spotlight on a brilliant new designer who is just starting out if she was seen in all the right places with someone the media love to write about,' Nick agreed.

'Don't encourage her!' Darcy pleaded.

'At last, someone who understands!' Clare sighed in a long-suffering 'nobody understands me' sort of way.

'But doesn't it rather spoil your plan if the guy in question bends over backwards to avoid the spotlight?' Nick wondered.

'These things have a way of leaking out—you of all people should know that, Nick.'

Darcy, who knew how ambitious her sister was for her business, was shocked by this display of casual ruthlessness.

'You mean you'd leak things to the Press…? Plant a story…?'

'Don't you worry your head about the details, Darce.'

The patronising comment brought an angry flush to Darcy's cheeks. 'I think you're getting a little bit ahead of yourself, Clare,' she bit back coldly. 'You haven't even met the man yet.' If she had her way that situation was not about to change. 'And there's no question at all of his staying here. Once Beth and the children arrive, not to mention Gran, we'll all be doubling up, if not trebling up!'

'I've thought about that,' Clare replied smoothly. 'You could share with the children in the attic room, and I suppose under the circumstances I could share with Gran.'

'That's mighty big of you.'

'There's no need to be like that, Darcy. I think it's the least you could do—'

'Whatever gave you the impression that I want to help you? I think what you're planning to do is callous and calculating…'

Clare looked blankly astonished by her placid sister's fresh outburst. 'But you said to Nick…' She was starting to think Darcy might be sickening for something—it wasn't like her to be so belligerent.

'I pointed out that Nick is a sexist pig.' She paused to glare at her unmoved brother. 'Which he is. But that doesn't mean I don't basically agree with him. What you're planning to do is cold-blooded and unethical.'

Clare's lips tightened. 'I think you're being very selfish. Mum and Dad invested a lot of money in my business, and I owe it to them to make it a success. I'm not trying to trap the man, but if meeting him happens to oil a few wheels, where is the problem?' Slow tears began to form in her lovely eyes; she sniffed and one slid artistically down her smooth cheek.

Even though she knew her sister could cry on cue, Darcy knew that it wouldn't be long before she'd be saying soothing things to drive that tragic expression from her lovely face. The pattern of behaviour had been laid down early on in childhood and was nigh on impossible to break at this stage in their lives. Somehow Darcy always ended up stiffly apologising and in her turn Clare would accept it and emerge looking gracious and generous.

'Maybe I don't have your lofty principles, Darcy,' she added huskily, 'but I do have fun...and so will he.'

The thought of Clare having fun with Reece made Darcy lose all desire to pour oil on troubled waters.

'What is it, Dad?' It was Nick who had noticed Jack's return.

'It was your mother.' Jack smiled a little dazedly at their expectant faces. 'She's coming home.'

Darcy closed her eyes. 'Thank God,' she breathed. Only just blinking back the emotional floods, she opened her eyes and saw Clare hugging their father while Nick, an imbecilic grin on his face, was pounding him on the back.

'Did she say why she...?' Darcy began huskily.

Jack shook his head. 'No, she said she wanted to talk. That's good, isn't it...?'

'Very good,' Darcy said firmly, hoping with all her heart that she was telling the truth.

Jack nodded. 'She'll be here tomorrow morning.'

Darcy had reached the point when she couldn't hold back the tears of relief any longer. 'I'll go get the tree in,' she announced huskily.

She was struggling with the evergreen when Nick joined her.

'Good news…?' He stood, his back against the garage door, watching her efforts and making no reference to her puffy eyes.

'The best,' she agreed.

'Personally I'm keeping all extremities crossed just in case.'

'A wise precautionary measure,' Darcy agreed with a tired smile.

'About Clare…'

'I don't want to talk about Clare.'

'You know she doesn't mean half of what she says.'

'The half she does mean is enough sometimes,' Darcy responded drily.

'Things aren't going as well as she'd hoped with the firm. I don't know the details, but I do know it's not good.'

Darcy's eyes widened in sympathy. 'I didn't know.'

'Only knew myself because she was in a bit of a state when I dropped in the other week. It does explain the conniving-bitch act.'

'You don't think she's desperate enough to…?'

'Sleep her way out of trouble?' Nick considered the idea. 'Shouldn't think so.'

Darcy was torn; she knew she ought to be more concerned about her sister's welfare than the possibility that Clare might find the solution to her problems in the bed of her own lover. Jealousy was not a nice feeling.

'Do you think you could give me a hand with this?'

Nick took the tree off her. 'All you had to do was ask. There's never a twin around when you want one,' he added, hefting it into his arms.

'And there's always two around when you don't want one,' Darcy added with feeling.

They were halfway up the driveway when Nick planted the rootball on the ground. His expression as he turned to face her suggested he'd come to a decision about something.

'I didn't tell Clare all the things I learnt about Erskine.'

'From a reliable source, no doubt.'

'It's all on file, Darce. Do you want to know?'

She shrugged her shoulders, affecting uninterest, while she was just bursting to shake the information out of him.

'Well, in that case…' he began, balancing the tree against his hip.

'I'm interested!' she snapped, grabbing his shoulder and spinning him back to her.

'Apparently the guy married his childhood sweetheart. Five years ago this Christmas Day she was killed.'

Darcy closed her eyes. Now she had the answer to his distaste of all things Christmassy. How awful to have such a powerful reminder year after year of his personal tragedy. Her tender heart ached for him.

'That's not all. She was pregnant…'

Oh, God, there was more to come! She could hear it in Nick's voice. Her eyes flickered open; she met her brother's eyes—not only more but *worse*. Darcy didn't see how that was possible but she waited tensely, her stomach tied in knots for him to deliver the clincher.

'A motorbike mounted the pavement—it was crowded with people coming out of midnight mass. They were holding hands, but it didn't touch him, just her.'

Darcy was seeing the horror of it; her chest felt so tight she could hardly breathe. 'He saw her die.' She blinked back the hot sting of tears; she ached with empathy. She turned away from her brother and fought to master her emotions. Losing a wife he loved and his unborn child—how did a person come back after a cruel blow like that?

'She died instantly, but he tried to revive her. When the paramedics got there eye-witness reports said that it took five guys to eventually persuade him to let her go, and, Darcy…' he touched her arm '…he made the biggest deal of his life on New Year's Eve. Makes you think, doesn't it…?'

'What are you suggesting—?' she began, hotly defensive.

'I'm not suggesting anything. I'm just saying that a man like that needs handling with care…'

Darcy's eyes slid from her brother's. 'Shouldn't you be telling Clare that?' she muttered evasively.

'Clare thinks she's a lot more irresistible than she is.'

'You only think that because you're her brother,' Darcy retorted. Jealousy tightened its grip on her—Reece wasn't Clare's brother.

Darcy tucked her hair behind her ears and stood back to get the full effect of her decorative efforts. She heard the door open behind her.

'Switch on the lights, will you?' she called without turning around. She gave a satisfied sigh as the tree was illuminated. 'It's a bit lopsided.'

'It's got character,' a very familiar deep voice replied.

Darcy gave a startled yelp and dropped the bauble in her hand as she swung around. 'What are you doing here?' Her body temperature seesawed wildly at the sight of the tall figure, as did her emotions.

'Do you give all your lovers receptions this warm and welcoming?'

Lovers. A sensual shudder rippled down her spine. 'Hush!' she hissed, reaching up and pressing her hand to his lips. 'Someone will hear.'

His disdainful expression was that of a man who didn't care what other people thought. Darcy would have taken her hand away, but he caught hold of her wrist and held it there against his mouth. The giddiness that had begun to recede came rushing back with a vengeance as his lips moved along her flexed fingertips, then equally slowly returned to the starting point.

Reece couldn't get over how incredibly fragile her bones were as he circled her wrist with his fingers. With the utmost reluctance he removed her hand from his lips, but not before he'd touched the tip of his tongue to the palm of her hand and felt her shiver with pleasure.

'And that matters…?' The shiver inclined him towards indulgence.

'How did you get here?'

He got the impression from the way her eyes were darting wildly around the room that she wouldn't have been surprised if he had announced he had materialised out of thin air. The truth was far more prosaic.

'I knocked on the door and was kindly directed this way.'

'Who by?'

'A twin; which one, I wouldn't like to say.'

'Oh, I thought maybe Clare had brought you?'

'I brought myself, and who might Clare be?'

'She's my sister.'

His eyes narrowed. 'Tall, blonde, persistent…?'

He'd missed out 'beautiful', which was tactful of him. 'You've met.' Of course they had—when Clare set her mind on something she didn't hang around.

'Not *met* precisely. I saw her through the window; she was knocking on the door.'

'You don't have a door.'

The bed to make love to her in, the door to keep out the world—he was a man who believed in prioritising.

'I do now.' A few phone calls had improved the conditions to bearable. 'I also have electricity. If I'm staying around I see no reason to suffer unnecessarily.'

How big an 'if' are we talking about here, she wondered, and do I have any influence on it?

'Why didn't you answer the door?' she puzzled abruptly. One sight of Clare would have most men tripping over themselves to let her in.

'I came here to escape people.'

Darcy knew what he'd come to escape, and she also knew that memories were not so easy to shake as flesh and blood people. It wasn't her place to share this with him—if he'd chosen to confide in her it might have been different, but he hadn't.

'I thought it was just Christmas,' she reminded him as with a grin she draped a strand of tinsel around his neck.

'Slip of the tongue.'

It could slip in her direction any time. 'Freudian…?'

'You tell me; you seem very well-versed.' His expression didn't suggest his opinion of psychoanalysis was high.

'This is Christmas.' Her gesture took in the room. 'And I'm people,' she reminded him.

He reached out and cupped her chin in his hand. 'You're a special person,' he contradicted firmly.

The breath caught in her throat. It didn't mean anything; there had only been one special person in Reece's life and he had lost her.

Darcy had promised herself she wouldn't allow herself to fall into this trap. When he wasn't here it had been easy to tell herself she wasn't going to see desire in his face and read love. Now he was here she had to keep reminding herself he was out for a good time and that was all; she had to accept that because the only alternative to not seeing him at all was even less acceptable—wasn't it…?

'Why are you here, Reece?'

An alertness flickered into his eyes. 'Here as in this

room? Or are we talking bed…life…?' His voice hardened. 'What's happened, Darcy?'

'Nothing.' Nervously she withdrew the hand he held and nursed it against her chest.

'Then why won't you look at me?' He took her chin in his hand and forced her face up to him. 'Look at me, Darcy,' he commanded. His eyes scoured her face, reading each line and curve. 'Someone's told you about Joanne.'

Joanne…so that had been her name. It struck her afresh that his perception was nothing short of spooky.

'Nick,' she admitted, half-relieved. 'I'm so sorry, Reece.'

'And now you want to comfort me, offer me solace and make me forget…'

It was hard not to recoil from the arid harshness in his voice.

'You'll never forget; why would you want to? I'm sure you have a lot of precious memories.' She could almost see the barriers going up—she had to do something to stop him retreating behind them. 'And actually,' she improvised wildly, 'I'm concerned about getting…*involved* with someone who has so much unresolved…' Her underdeveloped lying skills deserted her.

'Angst…? Baggage…?' he suggested with a quirk of one dark brow.

Darcy had the distinct impression he was relieved by what she'd said.

'I don't mean to be callous.' It horrified her that he found it so easy to believe she was that shallow.

'Don't apologise for being honest, Darcy.'

Ouch!

The lines bracketing his sensual mouth suddenly relaxed. 'Sorry.'

Her eyes widened. 'What for?'

'I get defensive.'

And I'm not defensive enough, she thought, staring longingly up into his strong-boned face—she loved every inch of it.

'I was afraid at first you might be the sort of girl on the look-out for marriage and children.'

It was coming over loud and clear that he didn't want either—at least, not with her!

'Me...?' she gave a jaunty laugh and shook her head. 'That's not on my agenda for years and years yet!'

'It's hard to timetable these things. Sometimes it happens when you least expect it.'

'Is that how it happened...with you and your wife?' She seemed to have tapped into some hitherto unsuspected streak of masochism in her nature. 'Sorry, I didn't mean to pry.'

His taut jawline tensed. 'Jo and I were as good as brought up together; her parents and mine were... You know the sort of thing.' Darcy nodded. 'She proposed to me when we were seven.' For a moment his expression softened and grew distant. 'I did the proposing the next time. Keep your eyes wide open, sweetheart,' he recommended gently. 'It would be a shame to miss a once-in-a-lifetime experience because you were concentrating on your career.'

The irony was exquisitely painful. 'You think it only happens once?'

'I *know* it only happens once.'

Darcy's thoughts drifted to her mother and Jack; they might not seem to be the world's most perfect couple just now but she had total faith in their love for one another. And significantly both of them had had previous marriages. It was hard to bite back the retort that hovered on the tip of her tongue.

'And if, like you, something happens to...?' she probed clumsily.

'Then that part of your life is over,' he bit back abruptly.

'There are other things...' his restless eyes wandered hungrily over her trim figure '...like *sex*.'

He was condemning himself to a very bleak future—not to mention herself. Despite the rebellion which she sensed building up inside her, Darcy had no control over her physical response to the smoky, sensual invitation in his eyes.

'And that's enough for you?' How sad—how horribly sad. Is that what she wanted to be? A distraction to temporarily fill the gaping hole in his life?

'You sound like my mother.'

A person that Darcy was beginning to have a lot of sympathy for. How did you help someone who didn't think he needed helping?

'It's not enough for me, Reece.' Fundamentally you couldn't change yourself, not even for love. It was a relief to recognise that she'd only be pretending to let him think otherwise, and, as tempted as she was to take what he had to offer, she knew that in the long run it would be more painful.

With a sinking heart she watched his expression shifting, growing harder and more remote.

'I thought you enjoyed uncomplicated sex.'

His tone wasn't quite a sneer but it was painfully close to it. Darcy flushed and lowered her eyes. Letting her mind drift back over her recent uninhibited behaviour, she wasn't surprised he'd arrived at this conclusion.

'At the time, but not later on.'

'That morning-after-the-night-before feeling—you're very frank.'

'It's no reflection on you, on your...'

His mobile lips curled as she floundered. 'Technique?' he suggested. 'Don't fret, Darcy, I'm not plagued with doubts in that direction.'

'You might be a nicer person if you were!'

'Would it make any difference to your decision if we were to put this arrangement on a more formal footing?'

'Formal!' she echoed, startled.

'Formal as in exclusive.' He hadn't planned to say this and in fact had been almost as surprised to hear himself say it as she appeared to be. Now he had, he could see the practical advantages of the idea—the idea of her being with other men was one he'd been having major problems with.

'As in, you don't sleep with anyone else?'

'As in, neither of us sleep with anyone else,' he corrected blandly. Darcy's eyes widened. Was that a hint of possessiveness she was hearing, and, if it was, what did that mean?

'That would be a major sacrifice.' Did the man think she cruised the single scene in a bid to add fresh scalps to her belt?

He seemed to find her sarcasm encouraging. 'It makes sense; we both want the same things…you're not at the stage where you want a commitment, and I'm past it.'

Darcy gazed up at him, speechless with incredulity. You dear, delicious, *deluded* man, she thought bleakly.

'Are you still worried I'm a loose cannon, emotionally speaking?'

I'm the only emotional basket case around here. 'You seem to have got your life on track very successfully,' she choked. 'Your work-life, anyhow.'

Reece's eyes narrowed shrewdly. 'Nick again…'

'He mentioned you didn't take any time off after the…accident.'

'Very tactfully put,' he congratulated her. 'A certain section of the Press never forgave me for ruining a great tragic story by not falling apart in public. I'm not comfortable with the role of tragic hero,' he explained, a spasm of fastidious disgust crossing his face. 'After Joanne died the Press had a field-day. The public appetite for the personal tragedy of people who have a high public profile is almost limitless. They wheeled out the experts to pontificate on the grieving process, interviewed every person I'd ever said good morning to…'

Darcy could feel the pain behind his prosaic words. It must have been agony for a very private man to have his grief dissected and analysed.

'And when you were working you weren't thinking.'

Reece shot her a startled look. 'That was the theory—it didn't always work,' he admitted wryly. 'After Jo's death the Press pack were their usual rabid selves, and my lack of co-operation only increased their appetite. Of course when I didn't oblige them by drowning my sorrows in a gin bottle they were even less happy. Chequebook journalism being what it is, any ex of mine can look forward to making a tidy profit—several have.'

Darcy's face froze. 'Is that meant to be an incentive?' she breathed wrathfully.

'Hell, no, I didn't mean you!' he exclaimed—she seemed to be remarkably lacking in avarice.

Darcy's hands went to her hips as she tossed back her hair. 'You'd better not.'

'I've made you mad, haven't I?'

'Whatever gave you that idea?' she snapped sarcastically.

'Let me take you to dinner; we can talk more.'

Darcy didn't want to talk more—she'd already had more *talk* than she could cope with. 'I c-can't go to dinner with you,' she stuttered.

'Why not?'

'Well, I've got a lot to do.'

'You have to eat.'

'And it's Clare's first night home.'

He looked palpably unimpressed by her clinching argument. 'The table's booked for eight-thirty.' He consulted his watch. 'That gives you twenty minutes to get ready.'

'Do people always do what you say?'

The lines that fanned out from his eyes deepened as if he found her futile resistance amusing—Darcy couldn't shake the uneasy notion that pursuit had a lot to do with his interest; perhaps his interest would cool rapidly once she'd settled for his terms.

'Nineteen minutes,' he said, not taking his eyes off her face.

'I don't react well to ultimatums,' she told him, smiling grimly through clenched teeth. 'Anyhow, you can't drive and I've promised the car to the boys tonight.'

'Nice try, but I've hired a driver.'

'Doesn't the driver think it's bit sus that his employer is sleeping in a derelict mansion?'

Reece's dark brows moved in the general direction of his dark hairline. 'I didn't ask him,' he replied. 'Eccentricity is only frowned upon if you don't have money, Darcy.'

'That's a cynical way of looking at things.'

'Whether you like it or not, that's the way the world works.'

'I don't have to like it,' she snorted.

'No,' he agreed, 'you don't have to like it—just me. *Do you?*'

The clipped abruptness of his question was unsettling, but not as unsettling as the peculiar intensity of his expression.

'Like you…?' Was this a trick question? 'I…I don't know you,' she blurted awkwardly. For a moment she thought he was going to push it, but much to her relief he dropped the subject.

'You're cutting things fine, and I'm hungry—in case you've forgotten, you did me out of lunch.' A slow, sensual smile curved his lips. 'Not that I'm complaining,' he added huskily.

Reece wondered if all her skin had turned the deep shade of crimson that her face had—he made a mental note to test the theory some time soon…very soon.

She looked just about everywhere but his face. It was while she was looking at the Christmas tree she thought of another excuse—feeble, but a drowning person wasn't fussy.

'I haven't finished decorating the tree.'

His attention was promptly diverted to the twinkling tree set beside the window.

'It looks as though it will collapse under the weight if you add another thing,' he commented after a moment's silent contemplation of the overladen branches.

Darcy rushed to defence of her efforts; it might not be fashionably minimalist, and it was light-years away from being colour co-ordinated, but every item that adorned it had sentimental value.

'Mum never threw away any of the things we made at school, not a thing; everything on that tree has a history.' She grabbed the fairy that had been gracing the top of the tree for as long as she could remember.

'There's a limit to how much *history* one little evergreen can take.'

There was also a limit to how much proximity she could take, Darcy thought as his hand brushed her shoulder—it was electric. The fizzling surge of sexual desire stole her breath. She took a stumbling step backwards.

'I can't…' she began stiltedly. Her eyes, which had been fixed on his expensively shod size twelves, started to travel upwards as if obeying an unspoken command. Long legs, more than a suggestion of muscle in the thigh area, and the loose cut of his tailored trousers couldn't disguise the fact he was aroused…as was she…*help*!

No benevolent force came to her aid. She could feel the glazed expression sliding into her eyes, feel the prickle of heat travelling over her body, and the worst part was being totally incapable of preventing it.

'Not touch—me neither.' His low-pitched voice carried an indecent amount of sensual suggestion.

She fought hard to master her seething emotions. 'I wasn't going to say that,' she managed to protest weakly. Her throat closed up as her wide, fearful eyes meshed with hot, determined green.

'You didn't need to.'

'That obvious, am I?' she asked, her throat clogged with shame. His thumb moved slowly down the extended column of her throat. Darcy, her eyes still melded with his, shivered and swayed far more violently than the overladen tree. She shook her head in an attempt to clear the sexual lethargy that had permeated her entire body.

'I'm not coming to dinner with you.'

His indulgence had a feral quality to it. 'Of course you are.'

Darcy bared her teeth. 'I'm not coming,' she continued trying to keep a grip on both her temper and determination—at the last second she lost her nerve. Telling him she was in love with him would have the desired effect of sending him running, but it would also leave her without a shred of pride. 'Because we have nothing to talk about,' she finished limply.

'Fine; we won't talk,' he responded amiably. 'We'll do this instead.'

Darcy closed her eyes as his mouth came down hard on hers, and the wild wave of longing that washed over her sent her spinning out of control. She gave a discontented sigh when he lifted his head.

Finally Darcy heard what he obviously already had; she

recognised the click-clack of the ridiculous high-heeled mules that Clare wore around the house.

'Darcy… Sorry, I didn't know we had company.'

Sure you didn't, Darcy thought as her sister made a graceful attempt to pull together the sides of the gossamer wrap she wore, so graceful in fact that they were granted several tantalising glimpses of what was underneath; Darcy didn't actually feel very tantalised—she felt as mad as hell! She cringed at her sister's painful *obviousness*.

As you could see right through the wrap and she wasn't wearing a stitch underneath, Darcy didn't see why she'd bothered to put it on in the first place. In fact, she didn't see why she'd bothered to put on anything at all—surely a towel dropped at the right moment would have achieved her purpose just as well. Reece had got an eyeful of the celestial body. She gritted her teeth and felt anger bubbling within her.

He was staring…major surprise—*not*! It was the moment that Darcy had been subconsciously dreading; now it was here it was even worse than she'd imagined. In that moment she knew what it would feel like if she accepted his offer and became—for want of a better word—his mistress. There would be the constant fear that he would tire of her, or cheat, or… No, she couldn't cope on his terms.

'Your hair's sticking up,' she snapped abruptly. And I mussed it up, she wanted to shout at her sister.

'Thanks.' Reece smoothed down his dark hair with his good hand and turned to smile at Clare.

Clare, who had looked a little startled by Darcy's abrupt tone, began to look more confident.

'You must be Clare. Run along and get changed, Darcy.' The man had the unmitigated gall to absently pat her on the behind. 'Clare will entertain me.'

I just bet she will!

'Darcy missed her lunch on account of me, so I thought

the least I could do was take her to dinner,' he explained smoothly.

'What's wrong with the way I look now?' Darcy asked mutinously.

It occurred to Darcy too late that to invite a man to look at her when he'd only just feasted his eyes on Clare was a bad move—the comparison was hardly likely to do her any favours. She'd invited the scrutiny, though, and she was getting it; it took all her will-power not to drop her gaze under the searching intensity of that raw sexual appraisal.

'Not a thing.'

A gratified glow spread through her electrified body, but she didn't let herself respond—she couldn't.

'Here you are.' Nick strolled past the frozen figure of his younger sister in the doorway, apparently oblivious to the electric atmosphere.

Darcy gave a sigh of exasperation. 'I suppose you didn't know we had a visitor either?'

'As a matter of fact, Charlie mentioned Reece had come here to snog you.' He picked up an apple from the selection in the fruit bowl and polished it on his jumper.

'He mentioned *what*?' she yelped.

Reece cleared his throat. 'He asked me whether I was going to,' he admitted. 'What was I supposed to do—lie?'

'Yes!' Darcy responded with feeling.

Nick did some more apple-polishing. 'I suppose you know you can see right through that thing, Clare?'

Clare shook her head like someone emerging from a trance. 'What? I...' With a muffled sob she ran, clicking and clacking, from the room.

'Was it something I said?' Nick wondered innocently.

'Don't be facetious, Nick!' Darcy snapped. 'I should go after her...'

'And rub salt in the wound...?'

'What wound?'

Brother and sister looked at one another but didn't reply.

'I'm taking your sister for a meal.'

Nick bit down hard into his apple. 'So long as you don't take her for a ride, mate, be my guest.'

'He won't be your guest, because I'm not going, and I'm sure you mean well but I don't need a chaperon, Nick.'

Nick looked from his sister to the tall man at her side, but didn't budge.

'For heaven's sake, Nick!' she cried, totally exasperated. 'I'm quite capable of taking care of myself.'

'Not always, you weren't,' Nick reminded her quietly.

'What did he mean by that?' Reece asked the moment they were alone again.

'I got involved with someone who forget to mention he was already married.' If he despised her for what she'd revealed he was hiding it well; maybe he was reserving judgement, which was more than most people did. 'I thought he wanted a wife, but he wanted a mistress...is this ringing any bells?'

There was a guarded expression in his lushly lashed eyes. 'Do you still see him?' he fired abruptly.

'Who?'

'The married guy!'

The implication that she would knowingly continue an affair with a married man brought a furious sparkle to Darcy's eyes.

'I don't know why,' she gritted, her voice dripping sarcasm, 'but once I've broken up a marriage the excitement goes clear out of a relationship.' Her icy blue gaze swept contemptuously over his face. *'You're as bad as him!'*

'I haven't lied to you...I haven't asked you to marry me...'

You haven't fallen in love with me, she wanted to wail.

'But you have asked me to be your mistress—not in so many words, but it amounts to the same thing.'

'But you're holding out for a ring?' he speculated scornfully.

Darcy shook her head and smiled sadly. 'No, I'd settle for a lot less than that.'

'Such as...?'

She met his eyes, her own gaze steady and clear, and, holding her breath, jumped in with both feet. 'Love.'

His big chest rose sharply. 'You know—'

'I know you loved your wife and you'll never love anyone else, or that's what you tell yourself. I think the truth is you're too afraid to look forward, so you keep on looking back—'

Reece, who'd been holding his breath, exhaled noisily. 'And you'd know all about it...'

'The only thing I know for sure,' she returned with an emotional catch in her husky voice, 'is that I'm in love with you.' There, I said it.

'You're *what*...?' For once his effortless air of command had totally deserted him.

There was no way she was going to say it again. 'You heard me.'

He opened his mouth, closed it again and then abruptly turned on his heel and left her standing there beside the sparkling Christmas tree.

She made it to her room before she started crying in earnest. This orgy of misery was interrupted by her sister's entrance.

'Go away, Clare!' she begged gruffly without looking around.

'Are you getting ready to go out?'

'The dinner date's off,' Darcy explained with a quiver of high-pitched hysteria.

'I wanted to explain about the way I acted... I had the most awful interview with the bank manager yesterday and...I didn't know that you and Reece...'

'There is no me and Reece!' Darcy sobbed, lifting her downcast face.

'Darcy, have you been crying?' Clare exclaimed, lifting the tissue from her own pink nose. 'Oh, Darce, what's wrong?' she cried, wrapping her arms around her sister's shaking body. 'He's not worth it!' she cried soothingly.

If Darcy could have brought herself to truly believe that, she'd have felt a lot happier.

CHAPTER SEVEN

'THAT'S it. I'm going in!'

Darcy caught hold of her sister's arm. 'No, Clare,' she hissed urgently. 'We can't barge in—Mum and Dad need to talk...'

'They've been talking for over an hour!' Clare pointed out. 'How long can it take?' she wailed, wringing her slender hands. 'Darcy, I just can't take not knowing what the hell is going on for another minute.'

There was a murmur of general assent from their brothers.

Darcy sighed. 'Well, actually,' she admitted, letting go of Clare's arm, 'neither can I.'

Nick placed his hand on the doorknob to the sitting room, where their parents had been ensconced since Cathy Alexander had returned home earlier that morning, and looked questioningly at his siblings.

Darcy shrugged and Nick, taking this as encouragement, pushed the door open. The twins and Clare pressed from behind, sending Darcy headlong through the door with a precipitate rush.

'Come along in, children,' Jack said drily as his family stood there, all displaying varying degrees of sheepishness and a uniform level of anxiety.

Darcy looked at her parents' faces and gave a sigh of relief—everything was going to be all right! Until that moment she hadn't known how apprehensive she'd been. Jack looked dazed—but good dazed, like a man who'd just won the lottery as opposed to one who'd just been told his marriage was over. As for her mother, Cathy was positively glowing.

'Your mother's got some marvellous news for you all.'

'Jack, they might not think it's so marvellous.'

Jack Alexander clasped his wife's hand as if he was never going to let go. 'Of course they will. Your mother is going to have a baby.'

His news was greeted by a stunned silence.

'You're joking, right…?' Darcy heard Nick say, his tone suggesting he was just as gobsmacked as she felt.

'This is no joke, Nick,' his mother said quietly. 'It was a shock to me too…'

Darcy recognised an understatement when she heard it. Take what I'm feeling and times it by the odd million or so… No wonder Mum bolted!

'…and it's taken some time for me to get used to the idea,' Cathy admitted, casting an apologetic sideways look at her husband. 'I know it will mean a lot of changes…'

'Not to us—we'll be at university… But you know, Mum, I thought you were past that sort of thing.' Charlie winced as his twin kicked him in the shin.

'She's only forty-seven, idiot!' Harry hissed.

Clare was the first to recover. 'Why, Mum, that's marvellous!' she cried, running gracefully forward to embrace Cathy. *'Isn't it…?'* she said pointedly to Nick and Darcy.

Her words seemed to shake Nick out of his trance-like state. 'It's a relief, is what it is!' he sighed, surging forward to join his sister.

Cathy looked at her elder daughter over their heads, and there were tears in her eyes. 'And you, Darcy…? Do you mind…?'

'Mind…?' Darcy echoed hoarsely. *'Mind…?'* She saw for the first time what Clare had seen right off—their mother was desperately embarrassed by the situation and seeking their approval.

'She means no, Mum,' said Nick, directing a playful punch at his sister's shoulder, which almost knocked her off her feet.

Darcy rubbed her shoulder. She knew she was grinning like an idiot but couldn't seem to stop; the relief was so intense she felt weak.

'God, Mum, it's so good to have you home. Now tell us, what has the doctor said…?'

'Yes, you'll need a hospital with all the facilities,' Clare began thoughtfully, perching herself on the arm of the sofa to let Darcy move forward and get in on the hugs.

'Because of my age…?'

'Age nothing!' Clare denied robustly. 'If it was me I wouldn't set foot in a place that didn't offer every pain-killing device known to man, and don't let Beth brainwash you with all that stuff about natural childbirth when she gets here,' she warned. 'Just keep in mind that it was Beth who ended up giving birth in the back of the Land Rover.'

'I never knew you were so clued up, Clare!' Darcy exclaimed. 'I'd sort of assumed—'

'Just because my career is important it doesn't mean I don't like babies, Darcy, and wouldn't mind having a few—when the time is right.'

That put me in my place and quite right too, Darcy conceded, aware she'd been guilty of pigeon-holing her sister.

The males of the Alexander family began to drift away as the discussion on modern childbirth got increasingly technical—or, as Harry put it, *yucky*!

The piped music in the lift was working its way through a Christmas medley and Reece was working his way through the enamel on his white teeth. Having taken the penthouse suite—thanks to a last-minute cancellation—he had no option but to endure the agony longer than anyone else.

He reached the foyer and was immediately spotted by the assistant manager, who hastened discreetly to his side.

'I hope everything—'

'Fine, fine...' Reece murmured without slackening his pace. He seemed genuinely oblivious to the fact that his tall, distinguished person was a magnet for numerous curious and admiring eyes.

'Will your wife...?'

This stopped Reece.

'I have not got a wife!' Without raising his voice above a low murmur he managed to give his words the impact of a blood-curdling yell.

It might have been that his ears had become supersensitive, but the more often he denied it the less convincing it seemed to sound. Perhaps that was what happened when you were forced to repeat yourself ad nauseam to disbelieving people all morning—first his mother, then his sister. The rest of the family would no doubt have got in on the act too if he hadn't instructed the switchboard to say he wasn't taking calls from *anyone*!

He didn't know what was worse—their initial reproaches that he'd slunk off to marry someone they'd never met and cheated them out of a wedding, or their bitter disappointment when he'd finally convinced them it was all lies.

He wouldn't have had the ear-bashing at all if he hadn't allowed himself to weaken and ring home to tell them where he was—and that weakness too could be laid at the door of Miss Darcy Alexander, with all her idealistic claptrap of families and sharing!

'No, sir.' The poker-faced individual couldn't stop his eyes from straying to the newspaper poking out of Reece's pocket which had announced very authoritatively that he was:

Billionaire head of the Erskine Empire secretly wed. Honeymooners involved in accident.

'Damn you!' Reece said without any particular conviction as he strode off.

'Where are we going, boss?' his driver asked as he produced the Mercedes—as requested, fully fuelled—in front of the hotel.

'We're not…I am.'

'The arm—'

'Is fully functioning,' Reece snarled belligerently.

'If you say so.' The driver, who had found his employer to be punctiliously polite, looked startled.

'I do,' Reece replied in a more moderate tone as he slid into the driver's seat. 'Take Christmas off.'

'Thanks very much.'

'And, Andy…' he picked up the newspaper spread out at the appropriate page on the front seat and screwed it into a tight bundle before pressing it firmly into the driver's hand '…take a different newspaper while you're at work.'

'Does this mean that job with your mother is off?' the young man asked with a rueful grimace.

'Do I look like the vindictive type? No,' he said, adjusting the mirror, 'don't answer that.'

'I wasn't going to.'

'If you can put up with my mother the job is yours,' Reece yelled over his shoulder just before the window slid silently down and the car drew smoothly away.

Cruising in the outside lane of the motorway, the man without a vindictive bone in his body contemplated the awful retributions he was going to visit on Darcy Alexander.

Having so-called 'friends' leak stories to the Press was an occupational hazard as far as he was concerned—even when that stupid kiss-and-tell story had appeared last Christmas he'd been able to shrug it off; this was different, though. He'd *believed* in those big blue eyes—hell, he'd even believed it when she'd said she loved him; that fact was largely responsible for the fact he hadn't had a moment's peace since. And now she turned out to be the sort of girl that ran to the newspapers with a fake but eye-catching story… Why…? Was she deluded enough to think that this would in some way obligate him to actually marry her…?

Before long he'd find out—even if he had to wring the truth out of her!

'I don't know what the fuss is about; in my day plenty of women had babies well into their forties.'

'Yes, Gran,' Darcy replied meekly, deciding on reflection that this probably wasn't the moment to point out the lamentably high maternal death-rate enjoyed by women of that rosy bygone era. When Gran was in full nostalgia mode it was better to let her run on…and on…and on…uninterrupted.

'If anyone had seen fit to ask my advice…but of course they didn't…'

'You won't believe how much little Jamie has grown, Gran!'

'Grown into what, is the question,' the old lady retorted, suitably diverted but not placated. 'I told that girl of Jack's she was making a rod for her own back, picking the child up every time he whimpered. Worn to a frazzle she looked, last time I saw her.'

'Well, she looks pretty marvellous now,' Darcy replied uncooperatively, 'and Jamie is a dear little boy, so why don't you stop being such a grouch, Granny Prue,' she coaxed gently, 'and get into the Christmas spirit?'

The lady, who was neither particularly old nor infirm, but a modern-minded, sprightly sixty-nine, sniffed.

'In *my* day I wouldn't have dared speak to my elders that way, young lady. You always did have far too much to say for yourself,' she mused, unable to totally disguise her approval of this character flaw in her granddaughter.

The entire clan, minus little Jamie, who, Darcy assumed, was taking a nap, was dutifully lined up to greet Prudence Emery. It was a noisy, boisterous occasion, during which the lady in question hid her pleasure by criticising the new décor in the room and offending Nick by falsely claiming he was losing his hair.

Taking advantage of a lull in the clamour, Cathy drew her daughter to one side. 'You've got a visitor, Darcy,' she explained quietly. 'He's in the sitting room, if you want to slip away.'

'He…! Who he…?' Darcy demanded, grabbing hold of Cathy's sleeve.

Aware of her mother's startled response to her shrill reaction, Darcy took a deep breath and tried to regain her serenity—actually she'd never been particularly serene to begin with, and lately not at all! Contemplating the way she'd been lately wasn't going to improve her mental well-being, so Darcy wisely decided not to go there.

With a self-conscious grimace she released her mother's sleeve and brushed down the creased fabric. If she couldn't manage serene she could at least rise to sane! People lost out in the love stakes every day of the week and they still carried on functioning as useful members of society; only wimps curled up in a corner and moaned about their tough break.

There wasn't even any reason to assume that this visitor was Reece, and even if it was that wasn't necessarily significant. He could have come calling for any number of reasons—none of which she could bring to mind at that particular moment. The 'he's discovered he can't live without me' reason was one she forbade herself to think about even in the hypothetical sense.

'Is it anyone special?' she asked, overdoing the languid

unconcern like mad to compensate for her previous behaviour.

'You tell me, dear.'

Darcy gave her mother a pained look; it was a burden having a parent who could read you like a book.

'I'd be surprised if he wasn't special to someone,' Cathy volunteered innocently.

'Does this *special* man have a name?' Darcy wasn't in the mood for enigmatic; her brain was aching.

'It's the gentleman who I believe was staying next door—Reece Erskine; a nice boy,' Cathy mused innocently.

Nice! Darcy choked with quiet restraint; her heart felt as if it was trying to climb up her throat. The anticipation rushing through her veins made her head buzz loudly.

'Right.' She made a vague fluttery motion with her hand. 'Well, I suppose I'd better... Couldn't you just say I'd gone away, Mum?' She blushed deeply and lowered her eyes. 'No, of course you couldn't,' she mumbled, shamed by her display of cowardice. 'The sitting room, you said...? I'll just go and...' Darcy made a hasty dive for the door; her mother was quite capable of asking any number of uncomfortable questions if she hung around any longer.

He didn't hear the door open, which, considering the racket they were making, wasn't entirely surprising. Darcy had taken the intervening minutes to compose herself sufficiently to avoid looking a total fool when she came face to face with him.

Her mental preparations had not, however, prepared her for the sight of Reece, sharply dressed in a beautifully cut mid-grey suit, crouched down on all fours with her small nephew riding on his back. It was only a matter of forty-eight hours since she'd last seen him but the wave of longing that hit her was so intense that for several seconds it drove all other considerations from her mind.

He had the sort of earthy sex appeal that a memory could

not fully do justice to, or maybe she'd made some subconscious effort to spare herself pain by playing down the details. In the flesh he was bigger, leaner and more good-looking than any male had a right to be—definitely more good-looking than a girl in love could be expected to cope with.

As she watched an excited Jamie grabbed a hank of Reece's dark hair and ordered him to stop in his baby treble. Reece promptly fell down flat on his belly, flipped over and with straight arms lifted the laughing little boy above his head. She only just stopped herself crying out a warning for his poor shoulder, or maybe she didn't because his head suddenly turned. Their glances clashed warily.

In that second all Darcy's hopes faded and died. The world had become an even more confusing place—why anger…? Well, at least I know why he *hasn't* come to visit—a look of love that was not.

'Hello, Reece; your shoulder's better?' She nodded her head towards his arm, unable to take her eyes off his face.

'Full working order,' he agreed, flexing his shoulder to illustrate the range of movement. Underneath the commonplace response she was deeply aware of his seething anger.

'Aunty Darcy!' Jamie cried, catching sight of his favourite aunt. 'Come and play with us.'

'Not now, Jamie, darling. Granny has arrived—why don't you go and see her?'

'Has she got me a present?' the little boy wondered with innocent avarice.

Darcy smiled in a distracted manner and patted his curly head. 'It's very possible,' she told him drily. As she spoke she was very aware of Reece agilely leaping to his feet, and the room suddenly felt too compact for comfort—far too compact to take all the turbulent emotions seething around them.

'I'll go, then,' the child agreed graciously. 'Don't go

away!' he added imperiously to Reece, who was smoothing his sleek black hair away from a broad heroic-looking forehead.

Reece smartly saluted the little boy, who solemnly saluted back after a fashion.

'You can play with Darcy while I'm gone,' Jamie announced in a spirit of generosity before he left.

A choking sound emerged from Darcy's throat as her cheeks fairly exploded with mortified colour.

Reece's eyes ran insolently over her slender figure from head to toe. A muscle leapt in his rigid jaw and disturbed for a moment the smooth, sardonic mask he wore.

'I'll pass, if you don't mind,' he drawled with languid contempt as he slid the loose knot on his tasteful silk tie up to his brown throat.

The deliberate insult made the colour ebb from Darcy's cheeks. An expression of hurt confusion appeared on her face as she watched him refasten a single button on his jacket with equal precision. This was the first time she'd seen him dressed formally; perhaps he donned a hostile personality along with the suit...?

Reece saw the hurt and the bewilderment—both were hard to miss; fortunately he knew what a duplicitous little creature she was, otherwise he might have been foolish enough to respond to the urge to kiss away the hurt.

The icy glitter in his eyes was pure, unadulterated contempt—to put it mildly, Darcy was disconcerted. She responded accordingly.

'Mind...?' she laughed. 'I *insist.*' She bit back further retorts; they'd get nowhere if this thing degenerated into a childish round of insults. 'You've come a long way just to be nasty, Reece...'

He thrust his hands deep into the pockets of his loosely tailored trousers and viewed her from under the protective shield of lush dark lashes.

'I've had to wait a long time to be nasty.' He looked pointedly at his wristwatch as if she'd deliberately kept him waiting—an attitude which struck Darcy as being perverse in the extreme, considering she hadn't known his plans.

Maybe he didn't like children? Perhaps Jamie had driven him crazy…? It wasn't likely, considering the fact the atmosphere had been pretty convivial until she'd walked in, but she couldn't think of anything else to explain his hostility.

'You met my mum…?'

'She was very kind.' So much so that it had been hard to maintain his crusading rage in the face of such genuine warmth. 'You must be relieved she's home. I'm happy for you.'

She'd rarely heard or seen anyone displaying fewer symptoms of happiness.

'I don't mean to be blunt, but why exactly are you here, Reece? It's not that I'm not over the moon to see you…' Irony was an excellent disguise for the truth.

'Like you don't know…?' he drawled.

Darcy had the uncomfortable feeling she'd walked into this conversation halfway through.

'I've not the faintest.'

He shook his dark head, regarding her with disdainful distrust. 'What I don't understand is what you thought you'd gain by it.'

Her bewilderment increased. *'It?'*

Reece breathed heavily, his nostrils flaring, before he turned abruptly away, dragging both hands viciously through his hair.

'If what I've done is so awful that you can't even look at me, it only seems fair I get to know what it is.'

He'd have thought better of her if she'd not tried to pretend, if she'd been frank about it. 'You want to play it like that—fine.'

Something inside Darcy snapped; this was the man she'd fallen in love with, the man she'd spent every miserable second they'd been apart craving for. The sound of his voice brought her out in goosebumps, the touch of his hand or, for that matter, any part of his body set her nervous system into meltdown, and here he was, treating her as if she was public enemy number one! Surely this couldn't all be because she'd said she loved him—surely walking away had been punishment enough for that transgression.

She planted her hands on the gentle curve of her hips and raised the angle of her chin an aggressive few degrees.

'Don't take that tone with me!' Unless he considered falling in love with him to be a betrayal of trust, Darcy's conscience was clear.

'What tone did you expect me to take after you fed that ridiculous story to that filthy rag?' he spat in disgust.

'What story?' For that matter, what filthy rag? She now knew that Reece, who might well be the financial genius everyone said he was, could mess up like everyone else. Human fallibility could be charming in a way, but not on this occasion.

He produced a screwed-up newspaper from his pocket and waved it in front of her. 'I expect you've had your copy framed. Did you get a kick out of seeing your name in print?' he asked, ignoring for the moment the fact her name hadn't appeared in the article.

'You can carry on talking in riddles if you like, but we'll get nowhere fast, and if you think I'm going to oblige you by being intimidated by this pathetic display, think again!' she flung for good measure.

Reece surveyed her through disillusioned eyes. 'You fed the paper a story about me being married—to you.'

The accusation was so ridiculous that she couldn't even be angry any more. 'Don't be stupid.' With a frown she impatiently snatched the paper from his hand.

'Page five,' he told her curtly. 'Have you any idea what havoc you've caused…?' he ranted. 'It took me three-quarters of an hour to convince my mother I haven't got married, and even after I'd managed to do that she still wanted to know what you were like…'

Darcy was bewildered but intrigued by these revelations. 'What did you say?'

Reece shot her a murderous glare. 'As for my sister, she insisted on giving me the number of the lisping idiot who designed her friend's wedding dress…! I wouldn't let that fawning creep within ten miles of my inside leg!'

Darcy giggled; it was inappropriate but she couldn't help herself, he looked so outraged. A blast of raw wrath from his spectacular eyes had her hurriedly spreading out the paper on the floor and squatting down beside it.

'You didn't make the front page—I can see why you're so miffed,' she mocked flippantly. 'I'm pretty miffed myself,' she added, solemnly quoting, '"Witnesses tell us that the distraught young bride temporarily separated from her husband was comforted by the hospital staff after she collapsed." *How wet!*' she exclaimed in disgust. 'I might sue.'

'Get in line.' It was slowly dawning on Reece that she wasn't reacting like the guilty party here—in fact, nothing had gone as he'd envisaged so far. He'd sailed in here, determined to deal out a retribution that was both swift and awful—the details of which he hadn't quite worked out—and he'd been taken to the family bosom and treated like a long-lost son.

Darcy tucked her hair behind her ears as she bent over the paper. The grainy picture didn't do him justice. Rapidly she scanned the rest of the print beneath. It only took her a few moments to digest the salient details. She sat back on her heels and lifted her face to his.

'Well, you've only yourself to blame.'

'Me!'

'Well, you're the one who made up that stupid story about me being your wife, and it was obvious that that girl on the hospital reception recognised you...'

She saw his eyes widen fractionally as he absorbed what she was saying.

'You're saying that *she's* the source of this story...?' My God, why hadn't he thought of that? It was so damned *obvious*. It made no sense...it was entirely out of character for him to jump to a conclusion the way he had.

Darcy shrugged. 'Well, let's face it, she's a hell of a lot more likely a candidate than me. If I did want my five minutes of fame I can think of better ways to get it than that!'

There was a startled silence.

If she'd been the sort of girl to gloat, now would have been the time to do it. The expression on Reece's taut face revealed he had accepted her explanation and accepted the fact he had egg all over his handsome face, and Darcy suspected this wasn't a situation he'd had much experience in dealing with. In her opinion a dose of humility wouldn't do the man any harm at all—loving him didn't stop her recognising the character flaws in his personality.

She held up her hand and after a fractional pause he grabbed it and hauled her to her feet.

'I might,' he conceded slowly, 'have been a trifle...*hasty*.'

'You weren't a *trifle* insulting and rude?' She withdrew her hand from his firm grasp even though every instinct told her to cling for all she was worth.

'I suppose you want me to apologise,' he growled belligerently, his colour slightly heightened.

'Grovelling would be a start,' she conceded, symbolically wiping the fingers that had moments ago been enfolded in his on the seat of her skirt. 'I thought you were supposed to be clever—even Jamie could have figured it out. I had no reason to plant a story; if you recall, I wasn't too keen on the idea of being Mrs Erskine to begin with.'

'I was under the impression that was exactly what you wanted. No ring, no sex—classic case of carrot-dangling.'

'How like a man!' she gasped contemptuously. 'I didn't propose to you, I just told you how I felt.' She glared bitterly at the outline of the broad back he presented her with. It struck her as representative of his attitude. 'I only wanted a relationship where both parties are open to the possibility of natural development. We're talking *possibility* here, Reece! Is that so outrageous? I suppose it is,' she mused thoughtfully, 'if you're an emotional coward.'

In the act of pacing over to the opposite side of the room, as though he couldn't bear to be close to her, Reece stopped and spun back towards her.

'What exactly do you mean by that?' he demanded, his pent-up frustration clearly illustrated in every tense, dangerous line of his lean body.

'You loved your wife, and what happened was a terrible tragedy, but it isn't loyalty to her memory that prevents you from having feelings for anyone else.'

'Is that a fact?'

'Yes, it is,' Darcy reiterated bravely in the face of his simmering displeasure—she'd given the matter a lot of thought and had promised herself that if she ever saw Reece again she would share her conclusions with him. 'You're afraid to feel in case you get hurt again—it's only natural for you to be wary…'

'So it's a simple matter of cowardice?' He released a short incredulous gasp as his dagger-sharp glare bored into her.

Darcy refused to be intimidated—after all, what did she have to lose by speaking her mind? 'After my experience with Michael I could have decided to mistrust all men, but I didn't.'

'You're an example to us all. You asked me if it's outrageous for you to be so uncomfortable with your sexual desires that you dress them up with socially acceptable labels like *love* and *relationship*.' He skimmed her pale face with a provocative sneer.

Indignation shot through Darcy, who barely recognised this translation of her earlier appeal to him.

'I'll tell you what's outrageous, shall I?' He didn't wait for her to respond but plunged furiously onwards. 'You playing amateur shrink... Of all the glib...!' The fire died from his eyes as abruptly as it had ignited, leaving a bleakness that swiftly delivered an emotional ache to her throat.

He groaned suddenly and, with the appearance of a man in acute pain, brought his hands up to his head. She watched his long fingers curl deep into his hair as if he was contemplating tearing out the odd fistful or two.

'God, but I hate the way you make me feel.'

Whilst she empathised wildly with his pain, she couldn't help but be cheered by this news—at least he wasn't indifferent to her.

'Sorry,' she murmured softly.

Reece lowered his hands. 'What for?'

'For not planting the story.'

Her neutral calm was beginning to irritate him deeply.

'If I had you'd have a legitimate reason to dislike me,' she explained. 'And that would be very convenient for you, wouldn't it, Reece?'

'I *do* dislike you.' There was a shade of helplessness in his strong face as he watched her catch her full lower lip between her teeth and gnaw thoughtfully on the softness.

Darcy shook her head. 'No, you like me—you *definitely* like me,' she added firmly, raising her clear blue eyes to his. 'And I think you're afraid you could get to like me more. That's why you skipped town.'

'What town?'

He sounded amused by her claim—on balance she preferred hostility. Amusement opened the possibility she'd badly misjudged the strength of his feelings. It had been a calculated risk to directly challenge him and she was beginning to wonder if it hadn't backfired; she might emerge from this looking a total fool.

'A figure of speech.' What possessed me…? Why didn't I keep my big mouth shut…?

'Have you always considered yourself irresistible?'

A wry laugh was wrenched from her throat. 'With a sister like Clare? Do me a favour.'

'Clare is a clothes horse.' Darcy stood, her mouth slightly ajar, whilst he casually dismissed her beautiful sister. His glorious eyes sought, found and clung to hers. 'You're a *woman*.'

The hoarse observation was uttered with total conviction.

'*Reece*.' Darcy hadn't even been conscious of moving towards him like a heat-seeking missile until his big hands came up on her shoulders, preventing her from pressing herself closer.

This close she could see the beads of sweat across his upper lip and feel the fine febrile tremors that were running through his greyhound-lean frame.

'You were right, Darcy, there's no future for someone like you with someone like me.'

'What's someone like me…?'

'Warm, giving…' His big, capable, clever hands left her shoulders and slid all the way down the smooth curve of her back before closing over the tight swell of her buttocks. Darcy quivered as hard as a highly strung thoroughbred and pressed closer.

'In that case,' she murmured huskily into his mouth, 'why did you just kiss me…?' Her head was tilted backwards, exposing the long, graceful line of her pale throat.

'Because I have no moral backbone at all.' His hot eyes

lingered smoulderingly on her slightly parted lips. 'And you have the world's most sexy mouth.'

'I do?' she exclaimed, lifting a hand to her lips and provocatively tracing the full outline. She could almost hear the satisfying sound of his control snapping.

'You know you do,' he ground out savagely before he kissed her again, bending her backwards from the waist with the raw force of the embrace. She felt one arm steal around her waist, hauling her upwards until their hips were level. His free hand slid under the hem of her skirt and moved confidently underneath.

The frantic flood of feeling generated by the intimate contact sent her spiralling out of control. She started babbling—she had no accurate recall later of what she said, which was possibly a good thing, but she knew it featured his name and 'please', and both more than once.

It was a major shock to her system when he suddenly released her and placed her back on her feet.

'I can't give you what you want, Darcy.'

She shook her head, refusing to hear what he'd said, refusing to hear the horrid coldness in his voice. Stretched up on tiptoe, she let her tongue slide along the firm, sensual line of his lower lip. A husky little laugh rolled off her tongue.

'You can give me some of the things I want,' she assured him, plastering herself sinuously up against him in a manner that left no doubt to her meaning.

'Darcy, stop that!' he rapped unsteadily as she slid her hand between the buttons of his shirt. He grabbed her wrist and firmly removed it.

Darcy gazed indignantly up at him as he moved her bodily away from him. The heat of arousal died from her eyes, leaving a bemused, resentful expression.

'You stopped!' she wailed.

'I stopped what?' he snapped, making unnecessary adjustments to his tie.

'Kissing me,' she elaborated disapprovingly. Her body had responded to the promise of sensual satisfaction; now it responded just as swiftly and equally violently to being so rudely deprived.

Reece's eyes slid to her face long enough to take in the sexy pout but didn't linger. 'You don't want me to kiss you; I'm not husband material and I'm emotionally stagnant—remember…?'

Darcy remembered but somehow it didn't seem so important any longer. Glutting her hungry senses on the taste, touch and scent of him was.

'What if I can live with that?' She caught hold of the lapels of his jacket and forced him round to face her. 'What if I want to be your mistress…?' This wasn't a perfect world; a girl had to take what she could get, she told herself, rationalising her about-face.

'I don't want you for a mistress, Darcy.' He delivered the uncompromising verdict with a stony face.

There was a period of total, disbelieving silence.

Darcy felt the hot blood rush into her cold face. Now would be the time to retire, beaten, but with a token degree of dignity intact—Darcy never had known when to quit.

'I don't believe you,' she whispered.

'You make too many demands.' She flinched as if he'd struck her. That look in her eyes was one that would haunt him to his dying day. 'You were right—I need a low-maintenance mistress, and frankly that's not you.' He had to get out of here before this bout of selflessness wore off.

Darcy's stomach was a churning mess of misery. Pride was the only thing that enabled her to lift her head and look him bravely in the face; he looked interestingly pale, she noted irrelevantly.

'I'm sure you're right.'

'Yeah, right,' he agreed with a noticeable lack of enthusiasm.

'It's probably best you go now; I'll explain to Jamie.' Perhaps someone will explain to me why I keep inviting rejection. Perhaps someone will explain to me how a person is meant to cope with humiliation on this mega scale.

'Great kid,' Reece observed flatly as she led the way to the front door.

Darcy, normally a besotted aunt, couldn't even manage a smile.

'So this is your young man, Darcy.'

Darcy only just stopped herself pushing his solid bulk through the front door and slamming it safely shut as her grandmother, who had an honours degree in making awkward situations worse, materialised as if by magic.

'This is Reece Erskine, Gran, and he's not my man, young or otherwise,' she explained quietly. 'This is my grandmother.' She pressed her back against the exposed stone wall in the hallway to allow Reece an uninterrupted view of her grandmother, and the support the cold stone afforded was actually quite welcome.

'Mrs…?' He looked to Darcy to help him out and wished he hadn't, she looked so desperately pale.

'Prue.' Prudence Emery held out her hand. 'You can always tell a lot about a man from his handshake.'

Reece wondered if it had told her he was the sort of man who played fast and loose with lovely young women just because he didn't have the self-control to keep his lust under control.

'Mr Erskine was just going, Gran.'

'I read that article you wrote in the *Economist*—the one about ethical investments; very interesting. Though I thought you were a little unrealistic when you said—'

'Gran!' Darcy wailed, unable to contain herself any longer.

'Well, really, Darcy!' Her grandmother was not slow to express her disapproval at this interruption. 'I don't often have the opportunity to speak with someone who actually—'

'Actually, Prue, I do have to be going; it was very nice meeting you…'

'Is he always so abrupt?' Prudence asked her granddaughter.

'Only when he's just had to fend off the amorous advances of stupid women!' Darcy explained before excusing herself.

CHAPTER EIGHT

'ISN'T this just perfect?' Clare exclaimed, holding up a cute baby-blue sleepsuit.

'But is it entirely practical?' Darcy wondered, fingering the velvet teddy bears.

Her half-sister gave a sigh of exasperation as Darcy diligently searched for the wash label. 'Does it matter? It's cute, it's gorgeous—I'm going to buy it.'

Darcy grinned. 'I give in. Perhaps we should pick up some of those nice little vests…'

'Nice *practical* little vests. You're hopeless,' Clare complained, adding the sleepsuit to their overladen shopping basket. 'Don't you ever just throw caution to the winds and buy something totally frivolous, or do something you'll definitely regret?'

Would falling for the wrong man qualify? Darcy wondered bleakly. 'Let's be really silly and get the pink dungarees with elephants.'

'What if it's a boy?'

'He can blame his big sisters for any gender issues that arise in later life.'

'While you're about it,' Clare said, catching on to this reckless mood quickly, 'why don't we go back and buy that dress?'

'I'd never dare wear it in public.'

It was only her sister's pushiness that had got her into the designer shop—it had taken the joint persuasive powers of Clare and the elegant assistant to get her into the dress. Strapless black and deceptively simple. Darcy was inclined to think their flattering reaction had been a put-up job by

Clare to boost her flagging ego—besides, there was no way she could wear something that could be fitted in her wallet.

'Who'd want to?' Clare scorned. 'If you play your cards right, it's not the sort of dress that would see the outside of a bedroom—private viewings only,' she giggled huskily.

Darcy's expression drew taut. If she thought bedrooms she thought Reece.

'Let's pay for these.'

'You're changing the subject, Darce.'

Darcy changed it some more. 'If we want to find a table for lunch we'd better get a move-on.'

The streets of York were crowded with shoppers buying last-minute gifts, but even in the mêlée the couple drew a lot of attention—they were an extremely handsome pair. This man was the rare breed that people didn't barge into and bustle, and the girl by his side benefited from the invisible exclusion zone around them.

'Hold up—progress check.' The girl placed her list on the broad back of her companion and began to tick off the list she carried.

'Mum'll love that pashmina. She'd love it even more if you came home for Christmas,' she added slyly.

'Kate, don't push it…'

The young woman straightened her felt hat to a jaunty angle. 'It was worth a try,' she explained with a philosophical shrug. 'And stranger things have been known to happen.'

Stranger things like her brother ringing her up two days before Christmas to ask her to help him buy Christmas gifts for the family. The fact that her brother was intending to buy Christmas presents *personally* definitely constituted strange, if not miraculous.

Displaying tact and restraint she wasn't renowned for, Kate had only asked, 'Why York?'

She was still, however, eaten up with curiosity to discover what had brought about this dramatic thaw in her big brother's attitude to the festive season. He did after all have more reason than most to be cynical and disillusioned about this time of year.

'Who's Jamie?' she asked, consulting the list once more.

'A kid I know.'

'How old is he?'

Reece leaned down and drew a tentative line about knee-level.

'You don't know how old he is?'

'Not old.'

'I know I make shopping look easy…but *really*, Reece.'

'I thought you liked shopping.' He looked nonplussed by her attitude.

Kate was unable to deny this. 'Perhaps we should take a lunch-break—*Reece*!' she called out, hurriedly grabbing the bundles of brightly wrapped gifts he'd left on the cobbled pedestrianised road before plunging through the crowd after him. If he hadn't been so tall she'd have lost him almost immediately.

'What on earth are you doing?' she cried, as panting, she eventually caught up with him.

Her brother didn't reply, and she'd have laid odds he hadn't even heard her—he was gazing with a fixed, hungry expression at a point across the street. She automatically checked out what had caught his attention.

'Oh, my!' she exclaimed once she had zeroed in on his target—a tall, willowy blonde dressed in an outfit that had 'designer' written all over it. A dedicated follower of fashion, Kate couldn't place the distinctive style. 'She is incredibly gorgeous,' she conceded reluctantly, 'if you like blondes.' She touched the deep copper tendrils of hair that artistically surrounded her face a shade defensively.

Reece, it seemed, obviously did like blondes—or at least

this one—because, ignoring her completely, he was crossing over the street with scant regard for the traffic flow.

'Heavens!' she exclaimed when she realised her brother was going to approach the young woman. This was a major departure for him! For the past few years Kate hadn't seen her big brother so much as raise a finger to make a woman notice him—of course they noticed him when he did nothing! 'This is not typical behaviour,' she explained to a startled-looking passer-by before she gathered up the parcels and resignedly followed him.

Kate's amazement escalated when her brother walked straight past the drop-dead gorgeous blonde as if he didn't see her and right up to the girl she was with, a girl that Kate hadn't noticed until now.

As she got closer Kate could see that the girl wasn't unattractive, and in fact if she hadn't been with the stunner you'd have thought she was a very pretty young woman, though at that moment she looked as if she wouldn't have minded being invisible. The way Reece was behaving, Kate didn't really blame her; he was her brother but even she could recognise he could be pretty intimidating on occasion.

Darcy retreated into the doorway as the large, life-like mirage moved steadily towards her. Her stomach muscles spasmed painfully and the blood drained from her face.

'Hello, Darcy. How are you…?' The mirage spoke; his voice was deep and vibrant, and it made the hairs on the nape of her neck stand on end. Either this was a cruel coincidence or he'd been following her, which, given the way they'd parted, seemed extremely unlikely.

Kate saw the expression on the young woman's face and her own eyes widened—she wasn't screaming for help, but she did look as if she was about to faint. Not strangers—not by a long way!

It was no surprise to Darcy that he was with a beautiful young woman; Reece and beautiful women went together naturally. She couldn't help but notice he appeared to have overcome his qualms about very young women because there was no way this redhead was more than twenty. Presumably if she was low maintenance he was willing to overlook the age-gap.

By avoiding directly meeting the bone-stripping blaze of his emerald scrutiny, Darcy managed to respond stiltedly.

'What a surprise, Reece; how are you...?' She was beginning to understand how relatively mild-mannered creatures could turn feral and dangerous if cornered.

'I'm fine.' A spasm of irritation crossed his patrician features. 'No, I'm not fine, not fine at all!' he bellowed harshly. 'In fact I'm awful.'

I'm not so crash-hot myself, Darcy wanted to yell back. She drew herself up to her full height; it alarmed her that, despite the fact her defences were on full red alert, her skin prickled with sexual awareness and it smothered her like a rash. After the emotional mauling she'd received at their last encounter she didn't fancy a repeat performance. The nasty truth was she didn't trust herself in his company. It wasn't as if she'd planned to act like some willing sex slave last time! She squirmed, recalling that awful moment of rejection.

'Well, don't look at me like that—it's not my fault!' she yelled. '*I* didn't run away.' She bit down hard on her lip, hating the *needy* sound of this last tellingly bitter comment.

Kate was aware that the tall blonde, just as curious a witness to this exchange as she was, had moved beside her to get a better view.

'Kate,' she whispered, thrusting out her hand. 'Sister.' She nodded towards Reece.

There was barely a pause before the other girl responded.

'Clare,' came the hushed, hurried response. 'Sister.' She nodded towards Darcy.

'I want to look at you…!' Reece announced defiantly. The line etched above his nose deepened. 'I need to look at you…I *have* to look at you!' he finished on a startled note of discovery.

Darcy was more shaken by this announcement than she was prepared to admit even to herself. 'Well, you've looked,' she sniffed. 'So now you can go away, and if you follow me,' she added rebelliously, 'I'll call the police. They take a very dim view of stalkers. *Clare!*' She looked around wildly for her sister.

'Coming, Darce!'

'Darcy, you can't go!' Reece began urgently.

I can't *not* go! Darcy ignored his plea and made a neat side-step around him; unfortunately his elbow caught the parcels she carried and sent them flying.

'Let me.' Reece joined her on his hands and knees and began to place the tiny items back in the numerous bags. 'We should talk…' The steady stream of busy people divided, leaving the couple to form an island as the flood moved around them.

'Talk…?' Darcy responded in a low, bitter voice. 'Aren't you afraid I'll embarrass you by doing something silly like offering myself up to you unconditionally…?' Gulping back the tears, she continued to feverishly ram tiny baby items back in the bags any which way.

For once in his life when he really needed to say something Reece was speechless. When you heard it put like that it was pretty hard to escape the conclusion that he'd been a prize fool. What had seemed like noble self-sacrifice now seemed like cowardly caution.

'What's the point?' she added, snatching the last item from his hand and getting to her feet. 'Nothing's changed.' If he'd denied it she might have hung around to hear what he had to say, but he didn't, he remained on his haunches, staring blankly at the hand she'd ripped the soft booties from. 'Come on, Clare.'

'Reece,' Kate murmured after she'd endured several curious stares of passers-by. 'It might be a good idea to get up some time soon unless you want to be charged with causing an obstruction.'

Prone to clumsiness, Kate felt a brief surge of envy as her brother, who, even in moments of extreme stress—and this was obviously one of them—was beautifully coordinated, rose to his feet.

'Kate, what do you know about babies…pregnancy…that sort of thing?'

'Well, I read the book Mum gave me, and I attended all the classes at school, but…' She paused; there was no flicker of answering humour in her brother's eyes. 'Could you be more specific?'

'How long does it take before you'd know you were pregnant?'

'Well, I suppose that would depend on when in your cycle you conceived, but I do know you can tell almost straight away these days with the kits they've got. Never had call to try them out myself but I hear they're pretty accurate.'

'Oh, my God!'

At moments of emotional crisis in her life Reece had always stood out as a comforting figure of calm authority to Kate. Now she was shocked to discover that even her self-contained brother knew what panic felt like.

'What is it, Reece? What's wrong?'

He raised a distracted hand to his forehead, his skin deathly pale and clammy to the touch. 'All those bags were filled with baby clothes,' he said in a voice wiped clean of all emotion.

'Then you think…and it's yours…*hell's bells*!' No wonder he looked stunned. 'Anyone can buy baby clothes—it doesn't mean she's pregnant. They're probably presents.'

'There were dozens of them.'

Kate wondered whether now would be the right time to say congratulations.

Reece turned to his sister, a zealot-like gleam of purpose in his eyes. 'I've got to go.'

'I thought you might,' she responded drily. 'What shall I—?'

'See you later.'

No 'when' later, no 'where' later; how typical, Kate thought, watching her tall sibling weave his way skilfully through the shoppers.

There were no signs of life at the Alexander house. Frustrated but not deterred, Reece pondered his next move—he could wait, but inactivity didn't recommend itself to him in his present frame of mind. He decided to drive down the road to the nearby village to see if there was any clue to their whereabouts.

There was a noticeably large collection of cars in the cobbled village square; Reece joined them. Leaving the car, he shadowed the handful of recent arrivals. Their destination proved to be a small hall with a tin roof set just behind the church.

'Two pounds fifty, please,' the large female at the door demanded, blocking his way into the glorified tin shed.

Impatiently he handed her a ten-pound note from his wallet. His impatient direction of 'Keep it' as she began to meticulously count out the correct change seemed to shock her Yorkshire thriftiness, but he got in, that was the main thing—into what, he wasn't quite sure, but instinct told him there was a strong possibility, given the scarcity of social occasions in the area, that Darcy would be here.

The place was heaving, but thanks to their height he spotted the twins almost immediately; their blond heads were easy to identify above the audience, who were seated in rows of uncomfortable wooden-backed chairs. He slid into the back row and waited.

He waited all the way through the infants' nativity play and the resonant recitation by a large bearded individual. His patience was rewarded when the choir trouped onto the small makeshift stage. In the front row, looking angelically sexy and terrified, was Darcy.

'You were marvellous, Darcy.'

'I think I'm going to throw up.'

'What you need is a drink.'

'What I need is several,' Darcy, whose knees were still shaking, informed the pushy cleric firmly. 'And, considering it's your fault I was up there to begin with, you're buying.'

Adam Wells grinned. 'Sounds reasonable to me.' He gave her a quick hug. 'You're a trouper.' With a display of sensible caution he moved away. 'Not still feeling sick, are you?' he enquired warily.

'That's passed, but it was a close call. I'll hold you to that drink.'

'How about now?' Adam suggested, looking around the dimly lit empty hall.

Darcy, who hadn't really taken the offer seriously, looked surprised. 'Mum and Dad are waiting.'

'They're not the only ones.'

Thanks to the excellent acoustics, the words uttered by the tall, sinister figure who rose from the shadows at the back of the hall reached the front with no problem.

'That's excellent voice projection you have there…?' Adam commented as the tall figure came to a halt just in front of the low stage.

'Reece Erskine.'

The vicar leant down to offer the newcomer with the unfriendly expression his hand. 'Adam Wells.'

After a pause Reece responded. A closer inspection confirmed his suspicions that this Adam chap was far too young and flashily good-looking to project the right sort of gravitas required for his chosen career.

'Hello, Darcy.'

Darcy's only reason for grabbing Adam's sleeve was a desire to stay on her feet. The expression in Reece's eyes as they rested on her slender fingers curved tightly over the dark sleeve suggested he wasn't considering extenuating circumstances—he was considering homicide! This example of male perversity brought a spark of rebellion to Darcy's face. It seemed he didn't want her but he didn't want anyone else to have her either! 'What are you doing here?'

'I'm a music-lover.'

Darcy snorted. 'I thought your opinion of my voice would have been a good enough reason to give the place a wide berth!' She stopped short, her eyes widening. 'Were you sitting there all the way through?' she asked hoarsely.

Reece nodded.

Darcy swallowed and went cold all over; it was just as well, she reflected, that she hadn't known that. The idea of Reece watching her made her feel ridiculously exposed and vulnerable. No, that would definitely have been one critical pair of eyes too many. She turned to Adam.

'Reece thinks I have a terrible voice,' she informed him, sparing an unfriendly glare for the figure standing just below them.

'I'm sure that's not true, Darcy.'

'It does lack a certain depth and power…'

Darcy took an outraged gasp. 'See, I told you! Who made you a music critic…?' she demanded, squaring her shoulders aggressively. The fact he was essentially right was no excuse in her eyes for his comment.

'But if you set aside technique,' Reece continued as if she hadn't spoken, 'it was the most moving thing I've ever heard.'

Darcy's aggressive stance wobbled. *'It was…?'*

'Of course, I'm not what you could call objective.'

The hunted, furtive expression on Darcy's face got more pronounced as his warm, caressing glance came to rest squarely on her face.

'You're not?' she squeaked.

'There comes a time in a man's life when he has to admit defeat.'

Darcy's heart skipped a couple of beats and she promptly forgot that only earlier that day she'd sworn that if he ever came crawling back it would afford her great pleasure to laugh scornfully in his face—at the time she hadn't actually expected the opportunity to arise.

'What are you saying, Reece?' she squeaked without the trace of a scornful laugh. She slid her bottom onto the edge of the makeshift stage and dropped hastily to the floor. A person couldn't hear something like what she suspected—*hoped*—he was about to say perched on this ridiculous platform.

For some inexplicable reason Reece seemed to find her action extremely alarming; he shot forward and clamped his hands around her waist, lowering her the last inch or so as though she were delicate china.

'You shouldn't be doing that,' he reproached huskily, as if she'd just done something wildly reckless.

Despite the distracting warmth of the hands circling her waist and the deliciously weak, tingling feeling that permeated her body, she had to ask. 'Why not?'

'I'd have thought that was obvious.'

The only obvious thing to Darcy was that she was destined to love this man for better or worse, in the for ever after sense. She shook her head in bewilderment. Amidst the emotional turmoil she clung to the tenderness she saw shining in his marvellous eyes—everything was going to be all right. Her vision blurred as she stared, mesmerised by that warmth, into his dark, strong-boned face.

'I'll let your parents know you're making your own way home, shall I, Darcy…?' Adam didn't act as if he expected a response—he wasn't disappointed.

'You should have told me,' Reece reproached throatily, running a finger over the soft curve of her cheek. His smile was strained as he tweaked a strand of her blonde hair.

'I thought I did,' Darcy murmured, turning her cheek into his open palm. He hadn't told her he loved her yet but surely that was only a matter of time.

It occurred to Reece that they were at cross purposes. 'What are we talking about here?'

'I did tell you I loved you…I even had a crack at hinting that you might love me too, but,' she brooded darkly, 'that wasn't a big success.' The humiliation of that occasion was still too recent not to hurt.

'Poor baby,' he crooned, placing a warm, wonderful kiss on her parted lips. 'I was an idiot.'

'I think so,' she agreed breathlessly.

'You should have told me about the baby,' he murmured, stroking the side of her diminutive nose with his.

Darcy shivered as his lips made sensual progress towards her ear. 'How did you know? Did Mum tell you?' she wondered, sinking her fingers into the marvellous lushness of his hair.

'Does she know? I'm glad you told her.' He hated the idea of her having no one to share the news with, no one to soothe her worries.

'Told her?' Darcy echoed, pulling a little away. 'I didn't have to *tell* her, silly.' She bit down gently on his lower lip before sliding the tip of her tongue inside. The judder that ran through his body was highly satisfactory.

'I suppose a mother just knows these things,' Reece agreed, breathing in the warm, fresh scent that rose off her skin and hair.

'Well, she was shocked to begin with,' Darcy conceded. 'But I think the idea's starting to grow on her.'

'And you, how do you feel about becoming a mother?'

'Oh, I feel...' Her dreamy smile faded; she stiffened. 'What did you say...?' A quiver of apprehension shivered down her spine.

'I know how you feel,' he sympathised, misreading her expression. 'I was pretty shocked myself to start off with, but I'm delighted, really I am.'

Darcy firmly detached herself from his arms. 'What exactly are you delighted about, Reece...?' A terrible suspicion was forming in her mind—and it was so horrible she didn't want to contemplate it. But she had no option.

'Becoming a father, of course.'

The suspicion solidified.

'You think I'm pregnant?'

His indulgent smile was tinged with a hint of concern; her skin had acquired a worrying, greyish tinge. 'Isn't that what we've just been discussing?' He pulled a chair forward. 'Perhaps you should sit down.'

'Maybe you should.' So this was what his sudden change of heart had been about—for some reason he'd got the idea she was carrying his child. That was what happened when you allowed wishful thinking to take the place of common sense! She felt as if a lump of ice was lodged behind her breastbone as she lifted her chin to face him.

'It might have been what you were discussing, Reece, but I wasn't.'

'There's no need to pretend, Darcy; I saw the baby clothes—I know.'

'You know!'

For some reason Reece couldn't fathom she seemed to find this comment hilarious. His expression was sombre and guarded by the time her wild laughter had died away.

'I'm not pregnant, Reece.'

'You mean it was a false alarm?' Reece was amazed at how bad this made him feel, but was determined not to let her see his disappointment.

'I mean that I never have been. I was buying the clothes for Mum—*she's* expecting the baby; that's what brought about her emotional crisis.'

'Then you're not…?'

'Not even a little bit,' she confirmed, shaking her head from side to side.

'But I thought…' His eyes moved to her flat midriff and the blood drained from his face. There was a lengthy pause. 'I did some jumping to conclusions, didn't I…?' he remarked ruefully. He didn't mention the degree of wishful thinking that had made him reach such a rash conclusion.

'You're not the only one.' Her smile was grim as she recognised the extent of her wilful self-delusion. 'I thought you came here because you'd realised you loved me—how silly is that?' She laughed bitterly. There came a time in a girl's life when she really ought to stop setting herself up for rejection—humiliation aside, it hurt too damned much!

'Don't look so concerned, Reece, I'm not about to hold you to anything you said while overcome by paternal feelings. Though actually I think you'll find you didn't actually say anything too incriminating.'

'I did come here because I love you, Darcy.'

Darcy backed away, evading the hand that tried to grasp her wrist. 'So the fact that you thought I was carrying your child had nothing whatever to do with it.'

His broad shoulders lifted; he knew how this was going

to sound. 'That was a factor, certainly, but only in that it acted as a catalyst.'

'So you mean you'd be here if you hadn't thought I was pregnant?'

The expression in his eyes said it all. At least he wasn't lying—that was something. Though it wasn't enough to make her feel anything less than deliriously unhappy.

'Not this soon maybe.' The cynical little twist of her lips escalated his growing sense of frustration.

'Don't panic, Reece; as entertaining as the spectacle of you trying to talk yourself out of this might be, I won't make you sweat. You didn't actually say anything that could be construed as a concrete proposal of any variety.' No need for that when I'm so eager to hear what I want. 'And if you feel a fool you can take comfort from the knowledge that I feel much worse.'

'I'm not trying to talk my way out of anything,' he grated.

'If you say so,' she drawled.

'I *do* say so.' She smiled again with faint, damning disbelief. 'Listen, Darcy, I was *happy* when I thought you were carrying my child. Don't you see what that means…?' he appealed, his taut expression urgent.

Her normally animated face was blank as stone. 'It means you want to be a father.'

'If it was that simple I could have done something about it years ago. When Jo and the baby died I swore I'd never…' His rich voice cracked and Darcy began to sweat with the effort of not rushing to comfort him—it was following impulses like that which had got her in this mess to begin with. 'Before today I thought the very last thing I wanted—other than to feel responsible for another human—was a child.'

His emotions when he spoke of his wife were obviously genuine, but anything else was suspect as far as Darcy was concerned—or at least her interpretation of them was. She could no longer trust her own judgement.

'I suppose I'm responsible in my own small way for this breakthrough.'

'Will you stop talking like that?' he bellowed.

'Like what?'

Reece took several deep breaths and when he replied it was with a calm he was far from feeling. 'I only want a child if you're the mother...' he said slowly, as if he was explaining something simple to a very small child.

'You expect me to believe that!' Darcy gasped, her face crumbling.

This reaction hadn't been the one he'd hoped for. In the face of her tears, his hard-fought-for calm deserted him totally.

'This is just plain ridiculous. I love you!' he yelled in a very un-lover-like manner as he advanced purposefully towards her. If words wouldn't convince her of his sincerity, maybe actions would.

'Don't touch me!' she breathed venomously, batting his extended hand away. She refused to be swayed by the flicker of pain in his deep-set eyes. 'I'm not interested in what you've got to say, not now, not ever!' She ran down the central aisle, knocking several chairs over as she went.

For a long time after the door had slammed shut Reece stood there in the dimly lit hall, thinking. By the time he left he had the outline of a plan in his mind.

CHAPTER NINE

'LET me get this straight,' Clare said, her smooth brow wrinkling in an incredulous frown. 'The man said he loved you, and you ran away? And this is because…you love him? Am I getting this right?'

Darcy hadn't confided in her sister in the hope of being mocked—where was a bit of sisterly solidarity when a girl needed it?

'He was lying.' The explanation emerged as hopelessly feeble with an unattractive hint of petulance. Even before she heard it Darcy had already been wishing she hadn't, in a moment of weakness, revealed the disaster that was her love-life to her half-sister.

'Don't talk!' Clare remonstrated sharply. 'You'll crack the mask. How do you know he was lying?' She picked up the damp ends of Darcy's hair. 'Have you ever thought of trying some of that serum that helps frizziness?'

'I like frizz!' Darcy snapped.

Unable to bear being the passive target of her sister's subtle but searching questioning technique for another second—first a hint on skin care, the next a 'Did you sleep with him that first night?' Darcy gave a grunt of exasperation and flung off the towel that was draped around her shoulders.

Her sister followed her to the bathroom and waited while she rinsed off the greenish face mask which had set hard as concrete.

'You won't get the full benefit—you didn't leave it on long enough,' she predicted as Darcy scrubbed at her tingling face with a towel. 'So what about Reece, then?'

Darcy scowled. 'What about him?' she said unencouragingly—problem was, when Clare had the bit between her teeth she didn't need any encouragement. 'I wish I hadn't told you!' she cried, throwing the damp towel at Clare's head.

'Let's say, just for the sake of argument, that he was telling the truth.'

Darcy buried her head in her hands. 'I've already told you he only turned up because he saw the baby clothes and got this stupid idea that I was pregnant!'

'So when you told him you were about to be a sister, not a mum, he did what any man who was only reluctantly doing the right thing by a casual lover he'd accidentally impregnated would…'

Darcy winced. 'You've got such a delicate way of putting things.'

Clare's grin broadened. 'He hung around saying he loved you…?' She gave a bark of laughter. 'Come off it, Darcy, why would he do that? If he really only cared about the baby he'd have been out of there as fast as his Merc would take him.'

'Reece has more style than that! Oh, don't look at me like that!' Darcy snapped. 'You didn't see his face when he realised—he was devastated. He was only trying to spare my feelings. If he was in love with me he's had plenty of opportunities to say so.'

'Perhaps he didn't know then?'

'I thought you were meant to be the realist.'

Clare shook her head. 'Listen, Darcy, I'm playing devil's advocate here because to be quite frank if you end up with him I'd be green with envy, and if you don't I might just feel inclined to… I don't suppose you could call it rebound if he never was in love with you.'

'You're so smart,' Darcy hissed. 'What about the redhead?'

'I told you, she's the sister. Go on—admit it; the idea of me making a move on your man makes you want to tear my hair out!'

'I'm not in the mood for mind games, Clare; I've fallen in love with him, that's no secret—*unfortunately*,' she added gloomily. It seemed that her love-life was the main topic of conversation in the locality.

'This isn't like you, Darcy…'

'What isn't like me…?'

'Wimping out isn't like you. You're not totally convinced he isn't in love with you, are you? Be honest.' She gave a crow of triumph as her sister's eyes slid away. 'I thought as much. You'll always wonder if you don't find out for sure.'

'How do you propose I find out?'

'Go next door and ask him.'

'What?' Darcy exclaimed, dropping the comb she'd been running through her damp hair.

'He's next door waiting right now,' Clare explained smugly.

'This is a set-up!' Darcy accused wrathfully. 'You've been got at,' she fumed. 'How much did it cost him?' The flicker of pain on her sister's face brought her back to her senses. 'I didn't mean that, Clare; I was mad. He's next door, you say…?'

'Waiting,' Clare agreed.

The shiny new door complete with a Christmas wreath swung open when she placed her hand on it. Chin high—Darcy didn't want anyone to get the idea this was one of the scariest things she'd ever done—she stalked towards the brand-new living-room door and pushed it open.

She opened her mouth to announce herself and it stayed that way as she took in the decor—actually it was hard to miss. Just about every possible surface had been draped with strings of twinkling, blinking fairy lights, there were singing Santas and clockwork reindeer, and the tree was so tall she decided it must have been erected with the aid of heavy-duty lifting equipment.

'Good God!' she gasped. 'What have you done?'

'Do you like it? All courtesy of Uncle Rick. I bought his entire stock.' Reece's tall figure moved out from behind the bulk of the towering fir. He was wearing dark jeans and a lighter cashmere sweater; the sleeves were pushed up to his elbows and she could see the fine mesh of dark hairs on his strong, sinewed forearms.

Darcy tore her eyes clear of this disturbing spectacle and focused her gaze on the very top of the towering Christmas tree. She briskly began to rub her own forearms, which, like the rest of her body, were covered by a layer of goose-bumps. She was incapable of disentangling the earthy sex appeal from the rest of the man, which meant she couldn't look at him and think pure, chaste thoughts.

It took her several dry-throated seconds to get on top of her steamy, impure thoughts.

'I take it you were working on the theory that more is better,' she remarked hoarsely.

'I was making a point.'

'If the point was you have no taste, congratulations—it worked.'

'I'm a changed man. I'm not running any more—not from anything.'

The same couldn't be said of Darcy, whose wary glance finally strayed to his face and refused to budge. 'Could you make that any more oblique if you tried…?' she croaked. If he wanted to say something, why didn't he just say it?

'I could have made it more tasteless, only they didn't have a Santa costume to fit me, which was a pity because they had this one number with strategically placed Velcro.

One quick flick and the whole thing was off.' He inscribed a sweeping motion with his hand.

The image his words and action conjured up reduced her to a stuttering wreck. 'That's d-disgusting!' she choked, going a deeper shade of pink.

'Ingenious, I thought.' He moved towards her, but his stride was lacking the flowing animal grace she realised she associated with him. It was then she saw what she'd been too self-absorbed to notice earlier—the screaming tension behind his mocking grin. 'So you came.' His eyes were acting very hungry as they moved restlessly over her slender figure.

'Clare can be very persuasive,' she croaked drily.

'Nice girl.'

'*Beautiful* girl.'

'Really…? I hadn't noticed.' His grin invited her to share the joke. It was an invitation she tried very hard to refuse. Reece sighed noisily. 'Listen, Darcy, I'm not interested in beautiful girls, I'm interested in *you*!' he announced forcibly. *'Oh, God!'* He struck his forehead with the heel of his hand.

Reece's relief was palpable when she started to laugh. The laughter didn't remove the high tension between them but it did reduce it slightly.

'Can we start again?'

She gave a jerky little nod and shot a covetous peek at his profile—it was perfect, but then she hadn't expected it not to be.

'Thanks. The thing is, I'm so damned nervous I don't know what I'm saying.'

'*You're* nervous!' The sneaky peek was in danger of turning into a transfixed stare.

'You look shocked.'

Darcy was shocked. 'I just never thought of *you* as….'

It wasn't the fact he was vulnerable that shocked her, it was the fact he was letting her see it!

'Human?' A surge of colour travelled along the slashing crests of his slanted cheekbones and his ironic gaze drilled into her. 'The rest of my life is hanging on my getting this right, Darcy. I think under the circumstances I've got every right to be nervous.' He dragged an unsteady hand through his hair, his raw frustration clearly evident in his voice and tense stance.

She raised her eyes slowly to his, and her heart began banging noisily against her ribs. 'Perhaps you ought to get on with it,' she suggested gruffly.

Darcy had the sort of optimism that wouldn't lie down and play dead for long. It was making a spectacular comeback at that precise moment and she was trying hard not to show it.

Reece nodded. He folded his long frame down onto the bed, and patted the spot beside him. 'Sit...?'

Darcy shook her head emphatically—if she did as he suggested they'd never get any talking done.

'You're probably right,' he conceded, apparently arriving pretty swiftly at the same conclusion she had. 'You said you loved me, and I ran away. I said I loved you, and you ran away. Have you wondered what would happen if we both said it at the same time...?'

Her throat was so dry she could hardly form the words. 'I don't waste my time on pointless speculation...'

He smiled; it wasn't a safe kind of smile.

'Neither do I, sweetheart.' There was a very predatory look in his eyes as he explained this—the sort of look which should have offended her sense of political correctness; hormones being what they were, it actually sent a surge of sexual excitement so intense through her that she felt dizzy.

'I reacted badly when you said you loved me, so any

scepticism on your part when I announce I feel the same way is kind of understandable—up to a point…'

'What point is that?'

'The point where you ruin both our lives, Darcy.' He paused as if he expected her to protest. 'I won't let you do that,' he warned forcefully.

'Then what are you waiting for? Talk. I'm listening.'

'I did come back because I got it into my head that you were pregnant…'

'Which I'm not…'

'…but that only speeded things up; I'd have come back eventually—how could I not…?' The wondering expression in his eyes as they came to rest on her made her eyes widen…she hardly dared believe what she was seeing was real. 'It just speeded the process up.'

'What process…?'

'The one that made me see that if you're a lucky sod you do get to be in love twice in one lifetime. Joanna died…' His head dropped so she could no longer see his expression, but she could see the strong muscles of his throat work.

'I know how she died, Reece,' Darcy cut in quietly. It was an awful feeling, standing there seeing how much he was hurting and being utterly impotent to help.

'Then you'll know she died and I couldn't do a damned thing—I was standing there and I…' At that moment he lifted his head, his expression more composed than she'd expected—as if he was telling a story and not reliving it, something she instinctively knew he'd done many times before. 'She was so damned happy about the baby—I couldn't do a thing to help her, Darcy.'

'I know,' she cried, dropping down onto the floor at his feet and taking his big hands in hers. She spread her small fingers out against his and she sealed their palms together.

'I was her husband; I was meant to protect her and I

didn't. There wasn't a scratch on me.' While staring at their conjoined hands, hers so ridiculously small by comparison with his, he experienced a great surge of protectiveness that was primitive in its intensity.

Darcy closed her eyes and a single tear slipped out between her tightly closed lids. Reece had scars—they just weren't the sort that showed.

'I never wanted to be in a position to let down someone I loved ever again. Can you understand that?'

Darcy opened her eyes; her lashes were wet but her gaze was clear and composed. She nodded.

'It was arrogance, really,' he conceded with a self-derisive sneer, 'that emotional-control thing. I was remote from all that messy emotional crap. Then you came along and you challenged all that just by being there—then to add insult to injury you used the L word; I was mad as hell with you about that!'

'I was mad as hell with myself about that,' she confided huskily.

'I didn't want to believe what was happening. But even I couldn't ignore what had happened to me for long, and I squirmed out of that by telling myself you deserved something better than an emotional cripple. I know I was brutal.' There was an expression of bitter self-recrimination on his face as he recalled the events. 'And I'm desperately sorry for it, but at the time it felt like the right thing to do.

'The truth is, Darcy, running away gets to be a habit after a while. In a way thinking you were pregnant suited me—gave me an excuse; I didn't need to think too much about why I needed to be with you. Didn't need to face up to my own feelings. I never believed in love at first sight—lust at first sight, sure, but not love.'

He hadn't known then that love came in many guises and not just in the form of a gentle, slowly growing bond. He'd finally come to accept that sometimes the strongest bonds were forged in fire. He just prayed he hadn't left it too late.

'It wasn't like that with…Jo…*sorry.*'

The man had just said he'd fallen in love her with on sight and he was *apologising*!

'I'm all right with your past, Reece—I've got one myself. It's your future I might get a bit possessive about.'

During the stark, shocked silence that followed Darcy felt his big body stiffen.

'Does that mean…?' he asked, his darkened eyes searching her face with unconcealed urgency.

Her fingers curled tight against his and the pressure he offered in return was so emphatic she almost winced. She only broke the contact in order to press her splayed fingers to either side of his strong face. He did the same thing to her, his own long fingers curling round the softly rounded outline of her jaw.

Darcy blinked rapidly, her head still reeling from his impassioned confessions. 'When you open up, lover, you *really* open up.'

'Pretty disillusioning stuff, I suppose…?'

His eyes didn't leave hers for an instant. Darcy could almost physically feel the waves of tension emanating from his lean frame.

'I suppose it might be for someone who has put the man she loves on some sort of pedestal. In case you're wondering—I didn't and I don't.' He continued to look blankly at her. 'Stupid,' she crooned lovingly. 'I'm saying I love you—not,' she added drily, 'for the first time, and I'm warning you, if you do what you did last time I'll…'

She never did get the chance to tell him what she'd do because the tight control he'd had on his emotions slipped. Darcy saw the fierce glitter of his emerald eyes just before his mouth came down hard and hungry on hers.

Darcy's arms snaked up around his neck as he lifted her

onto the ridiculously opulent bed and plunged deeper into the sweet, welcoming darkness of her mouth. For long moments they kissed and touched with frantic urgency.

'God, but I love you.' He continued to nuzzle her neck.

Darcy nodded in languid agreement; his hand was under her sweater, running over the warm skin of her stomach, and the other was fiddling with the zip on her skirt.

Thinking skin on skin made her dizzy and hot, but blissfully happy. In fact it was possible, she reflected dreamily, that this much happiness was illegal.

'Say you love me, Darcy,' he insisted.

'I...' His fingers chose that moment to correctly locate one shamelessly engorged nipple, and Darcy let out a long sibilant sigh of pleasure and threw one arm over her head.

Reece's eyes darkened as he studied the enraptured expression on her aroused face. 'You were saying...?' he prompted throatily.

'Was I...?' she asked languidly, forcing her heavy eyelids open.

He brushed the silvery strands of hair back from her forehead before kissing the tip of her nose. Their eyes collided and Darcy smiled a slow, languorous smile that oozed satisfaction—he loved her, he really loved her!

'I remember now. I love you, Reece.'

'Too right you do!' her forceful lover gritted back, a smile of triumph curving his sensual mouth. 'And don't you ever forget it.'

Somehow Darcy didn't think that was likely.

'What,' she asked, shooting a flirtatious little look at him through the spiky fringe of her eyelashes, 'would you do if I did have some problem remembering...?'

'I'd do this.' She let out a startled shriek as he lifted her jumper over her head and impatiently flung it aside. 'And this.' Her bra swiftly followed suit.

Breathing hard, he gazed, transfixed momentarily by the

spectacle of her heaving, pink-tipped breasts. The warmth low in her belly sizzled into a full-scale conflagration.

'Isn't that a bit...excessive...?' she wondered huskily.

'No,' he contradicted confidently. '*This* is excessive, and this, and this...'

'Menace me some more,' she whispered brokenly as he divested her of her last stitch of clothing.

'Like this?' he asked, settling between her parted thighs and thrusting up hard.

Darcy expelled her breath very slowly and turned her hot cheek against the cool pillow. 'Exactly like that,' she moaned feverishly. To feel him inside, all the way inside her, filling her so perfectly. 'Is there more?' She managed to force the husky question past her parched vocal chords.

She felt the laughter rumble deep in his powerful chest.

'As much as you can take,' he boasted—actually, it didn't turn out to be a boast at all.

'You know,' Darcy said some time later, 'I should be going.'

Reece's hand, which was stroking her hair, stilled.

She lifted her head from his chest. 'I don't want to.' She felt him relax.

'Then don't.'

'I wish I could stay, but there's loads to do for tomorrow and I should get back. Mum is quite likely to get an attack of superwomanitis, and it's important she doesn't over-exert herself.

'In that case,' Reece remarked, throwing aside the covers and exposing her toasty warm body to a blast of cooler air, 'you'd better move your lovely little butt.'

Darcy rolled onto her side and propped herself up on one elbow. 'You're kicking me out of bed?' she asked indignantly.

'You'd prefer a display of unreasonable possessiveness…?'

She laid a loving hand on his chest and tweaked a curly strand of dark hair. 'Well, a sign or two that you'd miss me wouldn't go amiss,' she responded tartly.

'I won't miss you.' The extra-hard tweak she gave made him wince. 'Because I'm coming with you.'

'You are?' she echoed, her eyes growing round with wonder.

'Unless you have any objections.'

'Are you quite sure?' she wondered doubtfully.

'A man could get to feel unwanted…'

'Oh, no,' she purred lazily, 'you're wanted all right,' she assured him, allowing her wickedly lascivious stare to wander over his sleek, powerful body. Her smile grew smugly content as he responded instantly and pretty blatantly to her teasing. 'I just wasn't sure you'd be into our full-on, no-holds-barred, traditional sort of Christmas.'

'I just want to be with you,' he responded simply.

There was such naked, unconditional love in his face that Darcy's eyes filled with tears of sheer happiness. 'And I want to be with you,' she sniffed.

'Then let's get moving before we catch pneumonia.' Darcy let out a startled shriek as he tipped her off the bed. All thoughts of retaliation faded from her mind as she lifted her head in time to see Reece, completely at ease with his naked state, strut panther-like across the room.

Reece caught her looking and grinned. 'If you really want to go, Darcy, don't do that.'

'I'm only looking,' she complained.

'There's looking and then there's what you're doing…'

'If you don't like it, put some clothes on.'

'I will, but not because I don't like it…'

It took them longer to get dressed than expected because several items of essential clothing had gone missing. The silky pair of pink knickers were eventually discovered draped over a branch of the Christmas tree.

'It seems a pity to remove them,' Reece remarked indelicately as she snatched them free. 'You have to admit they'd be a talking point.'

'I know exactly what I'm going to buy you for Christmas,' Darcy confided as he slid her jacket over her shoulders. 'It'll be a bit late, of course, but you won't mind,' she predicted confidently.

'Is it a secret?' he asked, watching the play of emotions on her face with indulgent pleasure.

'No, it's a dress.'

He laughed low in his throat. 'Is it in my size?'

'No, it's in mine,' she giggled.

'It sounds promising.'

'You'll love it,' she promised.

The laughter died from his eyes. *'I love you.'*

The memory of the lonely ache in her heart receded even further.

He bent his head down towards her and Darcy stroked the strong edge of his jaw. 'You know,' she sighed, 'I'm going to miss this place.' She leaned backwards into his body and gave a contented sigh as his arms drew her closer still.

'You won't have to.'

'How's that...?' she murmured absently as she rubbed her cheek lovingly against his sleeve.

'I spent so much cash on the place that I thought I might as well buy it,' he explained casually.

'You what?' Darcy twisted out of his arms and gazed up at him, a stupefied expression in her wide eyes.

'Well, I'm as flexible as the next man, but I don't fancy sharing a bedroom with the twins every time we come to visit your parents.'

'And are we likely to be doing that often?' she enquired

wonderingly. It sounded as if Reece had been giving the matter a lot of thought.

'Well, obviously we will be after we're married, and, as fond as I am of your brothers, can you imagine trying to get a baby to sleep with them in the house?'

'Do you mind backtracking a bit there...?' Darcy pleaded hoarsely. 'You did say *married*?'

'I know we haven't discussed it, but *obviously*... What did you think I wanted from you, Darcy?' he demanded, looking mightily offended by her response.

'A baby...?'

'Naturally I'll cut back on my work commitments for the first year or so.'

'Do I have any say in this...?' she felt impelled to ask.

'You don't want a baby?' He accepted the news stoically. 'That's not a problem.'

'Of course I want babies!' she exclaimed.

'Whose?' he came back, quick as a flash.

Darcy blinked. 'Whose what?'

'Babies.'

'Yours, of course.'

'Then you'll have to marry me!' he responded with a smugly complacent smile.

'People get married for that reason but not me!' Her words carried the cool ring of total conviction.

The warm laughter fled his eyes, leaving a defiant wariness. 'What would make you want to get married?' He thrust his hands deep into his pockets and gave the impression of a man ready to argue her into submission.

'Finding a man I didn't want to live without, a man I wanted to share everything with, a man...'

'Like me.'

'Was that a statement or a question?'

'You little witch—you really had me going there for a minute!'

Still holding his eyes, she thrust out one slender hand. 'Shake on it…?'

'Don't be silly, woman,' he cried, hauling her into his arms. 'We'll kiss on it.'

'We don't have any mistletoe.'

'Who needs it…?' he growled, tilting her head back.

Who indeed? Darcy thought, melting with a blissful sigh into his masterful embrace.

Harlequin is proud to have published more than 75 novels by

Emma Darcy

Award-winning Australian author **Emma Darcy** is a unique voice in Harlequin Presents®. Her compelling, sexy, intensely emotional novels have gripped the imagination of readers around the globe, and she's sold nearly 60 million books worldwide.

Praise for Emma Darcy:

"Emma Darcy delivers a spicy love story...a fiery conflict and a hot sensuality."

"Emma Darcy creates a strong emotional premise and a sizzling sensuality."

"Emma Darcy pulls no punches."

"With exciting scenes, vibrant characters and a layered story line, Emma Darcy dishes up a spicy reading experience."

—*Romantic Times Magazine*

Look out for more thrilling stories by Emma Darcy, coming soon in

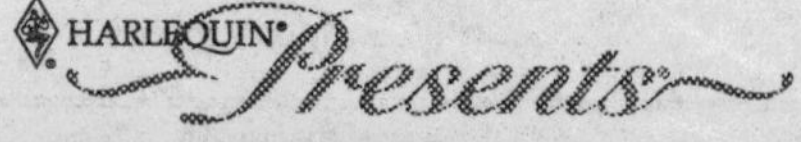

INTEMMA